THE GHOST IN THE GIRL

From the imagination of

TOM DELONGE

With

GEOFF HERBACH

Strange Times: The Ghost In The Girl
Copyright © 2016 by Tom DeLonge

To The Stars, Inc.
1051 S. Coast Hwy 101 Suite B, Encinitas, CA 92024
ToTheStars.Media
To The Stars… and *Strange Times* is a trademark of To The Stars, Inc.

Editor: Julie Scheina
Copy Editor: Jeremy Townsend
Managing Editor: Kari DeLonge
Consulting: Booktrix
Interior Design: Lamp Post

Manufactured in the United States of America

ISBN 978-1-943272-21-1 (Hard Cover trade)
ISBN 978-1-943272-23-5 (Hard Cover Limited Edition)
ISBN 978-1-943272-22-8 (eBook)

Distributed worldwide by Simon & Schuster

I would like to dedicate this book
to all the Ghost-Hunters, Bigfoot-Catchers,
Hoodily-Dink Wobblers and Alien-Snatchers
from here to the darkest shadows of Transylvania."

—Tom DeLonge

GOEFF'S THANK YOU'S:

Thanks to Jim McCarthy for setting me up with so many great projects. Thanks to Tom for imagining these characters I love. I'm grateful for all the youth adventure movies of the 1980s and to everyone at To The Stars for putting together this sweet, sweet book.

TOM'S THANK YOU'S:

Thank you to my family, Geoff for being so great to work with, everybody at To The Stars and my friends in San Diego that inspired the story.

CHAPTER ONE

This thing—our battle with the evil spirit Yankee Jim Robinson—has been going on for quite a while. Our latest encounter went down last night. Yankee Jim is weak right now and we want to get him before he gets strong again. So, we broke into the Whaley House with a high-tech ghost trap Wiz built.

Wiz's traps have gotten better and better since he started making them in eighth grade. This one used cooking oil, electrodes and a chunk of limestone his cousin sent him from Tennessee. Our plan was to sink Yankee Jim in cooking oil and fry his ass on the limestone. It was a good trap, except it was too heavy.

I led the crew through the Whaley House cellar door. (My name is Charlie, by the way.) We'd stolen the key from a tour guide earlier in the day. I carried a Magnum

1

flashlight—they're the best. They're strong and rock hard, so you can hit shit with them and they're really bright, too.

Wiz followed right behind me. He wore his gramps' old-school night-vision goggles and carried gear in a military backpack. He's skinny, but he won't let any of us carry it for him, even though the pack weighs a ton.

Riley followed Wiz. He's a big dude and he doesn't drop stuff like some of the others in our crew tend to, so he carried the Mel Meter, which detects temperature and electromagnetic fields ghosts generate. In hindsight, it's possible we should've had Riley carry the damn trap instead of the Mel, which is pretty light.

I climbed the cellar stairs into the Whaley House's kitchen. All was dark. All was quiet. The Whaley House is the most haunted place in all of California. Quiet doesn't necessarily mean good.

Mouse in his stocking cap, even though it was like 85 degrees yesterday, climbed the stairs and entered the kitchen behind Riley. He leaned over Riley's elbow and shined his small flashlight. "That thing's not working, bro. Not at all. No light. How are you going to see the meter?"

"There's supposed to be a light on the Mel?" Riley asked. He held up the meter. Lots of ghost hunters carry digital Mel's that look like handheld computer games. We know better. Digital doesn't work around ghosts very well. Ours is the size of a game, but has (I guess had, since it sort of melted last night) an analog thermometer and readout—this red arrow that rose when we got near electromagnetic fields. It did light up, too.

"We've been over this," Wiz said. "It only lights up if it detects something."

"Shh," I said to all of them. I focused the Magnum's beam on the door into the dining room. "This way."

Just then Mattheson made it up the stairs, struggling with the weight of the trap in his arms. So heavy. A small fish tank filled with oil. A big rock sunk in the oil connected to a car battery strapped to the outside of the tank with electrical tape. "Hey. You smell, like, a fart smell?" Mattheson asked.

"You always smell that," Mouse said.

I pushed through the door and walked carefully into the dining room. Darkness. Dust floating in the beam of my light. The others followed right behind. Once we were all in the dining room I held up my hand. Wiz stopped. But Riley didn't. Mouse didn't. They all ran into each other and some oil from the trap sloshed over the side of the tank and soaked the front of Mouse's shirt.

"Mattheson, you dirty bitch!" Mouse said.

"Just watch for Charlie's signal," Wiz hissed.

I'd stopped because I'd heard a creaking. A floorboard. Then, I heard something rustle, like a faint wind through the curtains, except the windows had to be closed for the night. There couldn't be a breeze. "Do you hear something?" I asked.

"What? What do you hear, dude?" Riley asked.

It wasn't a breeze in the curtains. It was a whisper, a voice. "Somebody's speaking," I said. "I think."

"Yeah, me," Mouse said. "All of us."

"Shh," I said.

And then, through rooms surrounding us, a ghostly voice drifted in the dark, "Hello, boys. You've come for me, I see . . ."

I was startled for a second. Spirit voices aren't usually so clear. This one sounded familiar, and I worried for a second that Yankee Jim had gotten strong again. I took a deep breath, then spoke. "Yankee Jim, you bastard. Is that you?"

Whoever it was didn't answer. The floorboards creaked more, though. I shined the light at the ceiling, then a hiss, like steam escaping a pipe, rose from the other side of the dining room. I aimed the light there. Nothing.

"Is that you Yankee? I'm sorry I called you a bastard. I just want to end the trouble between us," I said.

"Yes. We come in peace," Mouse shouted.

The Mel Meter in Riley's hand lit up. "Hey look!" Riley said. "It turned on!" The meter grew brighter.

"Are you here, Yankee?" I shouted to the air. Then I turned to Mattheson and whispered, "Get the trap going." He pressed a button on the tank and the oil emitted a weak, purple glow.

The Mel Meter got even brighter. Wiz stared at it. "That's not right. It's not supposed to do that. It doesn't have enough battery power to . . ."

At that moment, a large oriental vase slid off the fireplace mantle to our left. I spun and caught its movement in the beam of my Magnum. The vase hovered in the air and shivered.

"Check it out," I whispered.

"Holy shit," said Mouse. "Here we go again."

The vase moved towards us. The Mel Meter glowed brighter and brighter, until its green light became almost blinding. It began to buzz.

"What am I supposed to do with this?" Riley cried. "It's burning my hand! It's burning!"

"Yankee? Yankee Jim? Are you moving the vase?" I called.

A laugh echoed all around us.

"We're here to end this!" I shouted. "Manifest so we can kick your . . . bury the hatchet. Show yourself."

The vase floated until it was directly over Mattheson.

"Dude, it's totally going to fall on my head," he said, looking up.

"Talk to us!" I shouted.

The vase rotated as if tied by a string to the ceiling. The Mel Meter sizzled and sparked. Riley whimpered. Mattheson, holding tight to our glowing trap, stepped to his left, out from underneath the thing. The vase followed and positioned itself above him again.

"Shit!" Mattheson said.

"What do you want, Yankee?" I cried.

My flashlight and the Mel Meter both went dark.

"Uh oh," said Mouse.

"You know what I want," the voice whispered. "I want you dead."

The words hung in the air for a moment.

"Just Charlie, or all of us?" asked Mouse.

"Everyone, everyone, everyone," the voice hissed.

In the dark, the vase crashed onto Mattheson's head. Of course he dropped the trap and ten gallons of canola oil flowed out onto the floor. Then an alarm started blaring—I guess it took a couple of heavy objects basically exploding on the ground to set off the sensors in the house—and we tried to run, except the oil was slippery as shit. We basically ended up falling on top of each other, then crawling, slipping on our asses and knees to the cellar stairs, then sliding like damn sea otters down the stairs while that bastard Yankee shrieked and laughed and laughed . . .

We burst out the back door, got out onto the street just as the cops began to show up. We leapt on our boards and shot the shit off into the night, dripping oil behind us. Hope the cops don't follow that trail.

You know what? This crew, the Strange Times crew, is dope. We can pretty much talk to aliens. We've shared burgers with demons. We once rode on the back of a freaking sea monster! But we can't handle a shitty, pissy ghost named Yankee who is actually pretty damn weak at the moment and not nearly as scary as he once was?

We actually almost got him back in eighth grade. That's when he was strong and we were totally stupid! Well, we didn't come close to catching him really, but we did beat his ass pretty good. We defeated him! Then let him get away back to the Whaley House where he has a total advantage, where we've tried several times to get him, but can't, and one day he's going to get strong again, and he's going to come after me and try to kill me again when I'm not expecting him!

Jesus, I hate Yankee Jim so much.

Of course, without Yankee Jim there might not be a Strange Times at all. Yeah, really. If it weren't for the ghostly dude's murderous plan, Wiz, Riley, Mouse, Mattheson and I would never have gotten together.

We owe our crew to him.

Shit.

CHAPTER TWO

We were just eighth graders minding our own business, going through puberty and crap. We were definitely not friends . . .

Okay, I've heard this story a thousand times, but still can't believe the ghost girl somehow went to Mouse and Mattheson instead of Wiz, Riley or me. Anyway, she did, and this is where our encounters with Yankee Jim began, although we totally didn't know it. This is where *we* began.

That Tuesday night, just three and a half days before a big earthquake, just a day before these dudes and I all got stuck together in an eighth grade science project in Ms. Farhaven's class, Mouse and Mattheson skated into downtown Encinitas, looking for Natalia Carron. For some reason Mouse thought that Natalia wanted him to buy her a frozen yogurt. I know Natalia and I seriously doubt she ever even talked to Mouse. She's a very stuck-up girl. Anyway, that's where they were going, heading to Berry Happy Fro Yo on Highway 101, doing what they do, shooting in and out of cars, cruising down the middle of the street, not at all worried about the drivers shouting at them and flipping them the bird, laughing, and making fun of pedestrians, when things began to shift around them. Like the world began to go strange.

First a metallic smell rose in the air.

"Did you make that smell?" Mouse asked.

Above them the moon went yellow, then darkened to red.

"Whoa. That's messed up, man," Mattheson said.

A blue fog slid like a dead man's fingers from the side streets.

"What is that shit?" Mattheson asked.

The traffic disappeared into a haze.

"Shit. Jesus," Mouse cried.

The streetlights flickered and buzzed. And then a girl—the palest girl in the universe—appeared in front of them, forming out of thin air. Her blonde hair glowed in a single streetlight. Fog curled around her, over her, then broke as she stepped towards them, her ghost girl eyes wide.

"Ho-ho-holy shit," Mouse said. He skated slow now.

"You two stop," the girl said.

Mattheson fell and cracked his big forehead on the street.

Mouse skidded, almost fell, but managed to hold his balance just a foot from where she stood. He looked up into this girl's face, his mouth hanging open, his eyes popped with fright. The girl leaned toward him and breathed ice-cold breath on his cheek.

"Cold?" Mouse said.

"You don't smell right," she whispered.

Mouse almost peed, but pinched and tucked.

"So, okay," the girl said. "I'm here, boy. I know you've been expecting me. Are you going to help?"

"Help?" Mouse whispered.

"Help!" the girl shouted. "I said help! That's why I've been in your dreams!"

"I . . . I don't remember dreams," Mouse said.

The girl frowned. "Wait. You're not very spongy, are you?"

"What do you mean?" Mouse asked, chin quivering.

"Weird." The girl stood up straight. She reached down and pulled large plastic nerd glasses out of her skirt pocket and put them on her face. She looked close at Mouse. "Is today Wednesday?" she asked.

"No. Tuesday. It's Tuesday, girl," Mouse said.

The ghost girl sighed and shook her head. "Oh dang it! I'm not even supposed to be here. And you? Are you even you? Dang! You would not believe how much battery I had to suck to make all this happen."

"Suck battery?" Mouse asked.

"It's not even Wednesday!" the girl said to the air. "I have to come back tomorrow, I guess. Dang it!" And then, just as fast as she appeared, she was gone.

Mattheson pushed himself up. He stood next to Mouse and peered into the rolling fog. He said, "Who . . . who was that fine-ass nerd girl?"

"A super-hot nerd ghost," Mouse whispered.

But then it was like someone threw a light switch, the fog disappeared, the world turned normal, which meant cars flew by them on their left and one barreled towards them. It slammed on its brakes, honked like a deranged goose. Mouse and Mattheson grabbed each other and screamed like little girls.

That's how I imagine it, anyway.

Most people would be completely scared and destroyed if they had that experience, right? Most people would think they were going insane if a ghost shut down the city around them and breathed ice on their cheek. But not Mouse. He wasn't scared at all.

The next day in school he kept reminding Mattheson (and he literally had to remind Mattheson of the ghost, because Mattheson watched five episodes of *The* FREAKING *Gilmore Girls* with his mom after he got home and totally forgot the whole thing happened—that's Mattheson for you!) that it was Wednesday and Wednesday was the "right" day and that the nerd ghost girl would be back.

"Today's the day she will return and take me to the other world."

"Maybe, dude," Mattheson said, a little confused at first. "Maybe you should hide?"

"No," Mouse said. "If she comes for me, I must go."

"Dope," Mattheson said. "Maybe she has some fine ghost friends who want to ride around in their ghost Jeep and go out to the beach to do the ghost humpty?"

"Probably," Mouse nodded. "I'd be willing to put money on it."

In science class that day, Mouse set out to recreate the ghost girl's fine ass by using balloons and papier mâché. I sat alone at the next table over. I watched them make that ass. I have to admit it was a pretty good-looking ass.

But the ghost girl wasn't just mistaken about what day to show up, she'd harassed the wrong dudes all together.

Okay, you probably don't know this, but there are tunnels, almost impossible to access (believe me, we've tried to find our way back in), running under all of Southern California. These tunnels are filled with spirits and shreds and demons, all forms of disembodied one-time human energy. Down there in those tunnels, the ghost girl had heard echoes (that's what she called them, "echoes") about my dad and me and even some weird prophecy about me and a kid named Wiz and especially a spongy kid named Riley and so what does she do? She pops up out of the earth on the wrong day and scares the crap out of the only two guys in our science group who she'd actually heard nothing about!

It was supposed to be Riley. That's who she was looking for. That's what we found out later. And Riley is spongy, it's true. But, if I were the ghost girl, I would've gone to Wiz first.

Yeah. That ghost nerd girl's first point of contact should have been the skinny son of a Navy physicist. Why? Because Wiz could actually help. He was the one with access to the proper technology, to the proper smarts. He was the one who quickly figured out how to build Shadow zappers and spirit traps that might capture the things that chased. But instead of going to Wiz, instead of finding the spongy one, Riley, she accidentally made contact with Mouse and Mattheson, who responded by making a model of her butt in papier mâché. Good going ghost girl.

Here's what I don't get. She did somehow know all the Strange Times dudes were connected even before we were connected. Can ghosts see into the future? They do seem to get a sense of what's coming. How? No idea. Strange Times will have to research that at some point.

On the Tuesday she scared Mouse and Mattheson, Wiz, for instance, had nothing to do with any of us, yet. In fact, he had no friends to speak of, to be honest. First issue: the dude used to be so weird. He read steampunk shit and he walked around school wearing aviator goggles and a long scarf. Second issue: dude didn't have time for kids even though he was barely fourteen. He spent his nights and weekends building gadgets with his grandfather. Gramps, who lives in a giant shed in Wiz's backyard, was an army engineer in Vietnam. He and Wiz built so much cool shit. They even made a helicopter out of an old lawn mower (Mouse crashed it last year, but it did fly). His years of isolation were about to come to an end, though.

That very same Tuesday night, at almost the exact same time the ghost girl rose from the dead in front of Mouse and Mattheson, Wiz's dad sat him down in the living room and threatened to send him to military school if he didn't make any friends his age.

"What? You have got to be kidding me," Wiz said. "Why?"

"I'm not kidding. I'm dead serious," Mr. Wisniewski had said, pointing his big finger in Wiz's skinny face.

"But I get good grades and I don't get in trouble and I never do anything wrong," Wiz said.

"That's all part of the problem, isn't it?" Mr. Wisniewski said. "You need to learn how to be a man and that means you have to act like a boy."

Wiz's heart just clanged in his chest. His dad is a first class bag of dicks. Wiz knew he'd actually send Wiz to military school without a second thought. "I don't know what to do," Wiz said.

"Make some friends," his dad said. "Act like a normal human being."

"I have friends. A friend. Gramps," Wiz said.

"I mean real friends. Otherwise the military is going to teach you how to interact with people. Do you understand?" Wiz's dad said.

Poor Wiz nodded.

And so, the next day, all red-faced and filled with bad energy, Wiz set out to make real friends with real human beings, because he did not want to be sent away to some terrible school, sent away from his mom and his gramps.

During first hour, he made a chart in his idea notebook (he carries this rad notebook around everywhere, filled with scientific sketches of various flying machines and, these days, paranormal traps and sensors). On the chart, he determined that his best shot at making friends with "real human beings" would be in Earth Science, which was a required course for all us eighth graders. It was one of only two classes during the day where the nerd kids were pulled from the gifted wing of the building and placed in the slobbering maw of the general student body. (The other one was gym, and what was he going to do, make friends while everyone was changing into their gym shorts? "Hey, looking good, Keegan!")

Wiz hated Earth Science. The class was so far below his abilities, he was bored stupid. Also it was completely filled with goons and reprobates. (Did you consider me a goon or a reprobate, buddy?)

Except, weren't goons and reprobates "real human beings," the exact type of person his dad would want him to hang with? He circled the class on his chart in red. He whispered, "Best opportunity, Wizard."

It was a huge day for everyone involved. That afternoon in Earth Science Ms. Farhaven announced the Science Fair Project. "Fully twenty percent of your grade for the semester will come from this project," Ms. Farhaven had said.

Wiz sat in the corner and eyeballed the room. I actually watched him, because I was having friend problems of my own, and wondered if maybe I could work with him. He didn't look at me at all. He quickly focused on Mouse and Mattheson who had just been told they had to work by themselves and had been sent to a table in the back as punishment for not listening and for building the "ghost" ass out of balloons and plaster.

Ms. Farhaven circled the room as she talked. She stared down at the ghost ass and shook her head. "You'll provide a visual presentation and a group report, both of which you'll show to a panel of judges. You have TWO WEEKS to work! This is a huge percentage of your semester grade, so choose your workmates wisely!"

I snapped my fingers, trying to get Wiz's attention. He wouldn't look at me. He stared at the laughing Mouse and Mattheson (Mouse wore his dirty stocking cap and Mattheson had a large Band-Aid on his forehead from falling off his skateboard). Wiz seemed to focus for a moment on their ridiculous plaster-and-balloon ass.

And then he slowly raised his hand.

"Yes, Wizard?" Ms. Farhaven asked.

"Um. Well. I know you said they have to work by themselves, but I think I'd like to work with those guys." He pointed at Mouse and Mattheson. "I think I'd have a generally favorable impact on their academic pursuits."

Ms. Farhaven cocked her head to the side. "Oh. Are you sure?" she asked.

I heard Mattheson whisper, "No, I don't want to hang with a dork."

"Shut up. This is dopeness, dude," Mouse whispered back. "He'll do all the work."

"Oh!" Mattheson whispered.

Wiz stared at the idiots. "Yes. I'm sure," he said.

"Oh, yes, Ms. Farhaven!" Mattheson said. "We would like to take Wiz in our group."

"Indeed," Mouse said, "We would be very honored to have him be part of the team."

"Your funeral, Wiz," Ms. Farhaven said.

"It's going to be really good, I'm sure," Wiz said. "Really good."

I was shocked, pals. If Wiz worked with the fools, who would I team up with? Pretty much everyone hated me; even the new kid, fat boy Riley, seemed to. And, shit, I had almost been pulverized standing up for the dude!

Who could I work with?

CHAPTER THREE

I was not a happy boy back in the spring of eighth grade. Not at all. In the fall, I could've been in any damn science group I wanted. I played baseball and basketball and all those dudes were my friends, even the total douche sacks. The ladies thought I was a stud, which I would contend remains factual, even if they don't think so anymore. Truth is, I'd always been a little weird, but being good at sports covered it up. And things were okay at the beginning of eighth grade, except for my dad.

He was an Air Force pilot. That's what he'd done my whole life. That didn't stop him from being weird and funny, from having time to play with me, my sister and my brother. He took us on trips, to baseball games, out hiking. But, right before eighth grade, he was moved to a top secret program. He began to go on longer and longer missions. His health started to get worse, like the color drained from his skin and his hair turned gray. He got skinny, too. He stopped doing anything with us. When he was home, he was asleep or bent over his laptop working. Mom got pissed at him, shouted at him to talk to his superiors, get help, but he just said, "This is too important," and the Air Force kept sending him away. Then, in December, he didn't come back. My mom called everyone she could think of in the Air Force, but no one had information. She finally called the Pentagon and threatened to go to the press! That night a man in a black suit showed up at our house. He said it was imperative (that's the word he used: imperative) that we maintain with neighbors, friends, teachers, and everybody that Dad was fine, just continuing to work.

"But where the hell is he?" Mom shouted.

"We're not at liberty to say," the man said.

"Is Dad dead?" I cried.

"We aren't ready to make that determination. We have lost contact, however," the man said. Then he turned to my mom. "In the short term, it is imperative that you maintain that he is simply working. Do you understand? Lives are at stake."

My mom told the man to stick it in his ass. But, after he was gone, she told us to do what the man said, to keep all of this secret. Because of Dad's missions and his sickness, I was already turning into a piece of crap (it was like I drained of energy and happiness while he did). With the news that he was missing, I hit the damn wall. School went to shit. I stopped talking, stopped studying. I quit basketball because it seemed stupid and pointless, which pissed off the douche sacks. The coach sent me to the school counselor. She asked a bunch of questions about my home life. I couldn't explain anything, nothing about Dad. The man in the black suit said, *Lives are at stake . . .* I just shrugged. The counselor called in my mom. She just shrugged. What were we supposed to do? I had to keep going to school even though I didn't want to talk to anybody.

To be perfectly honest, I still have a hard time sleeping. I still hear Dad's voice in my head, still think it's him when the phone rings or when a car pulls into the driveway at night.

Anyway, by that spring, I'd turned into one freaky-ass loner. One edgy, weird, loner.

I also got super sensitive about some kinds of jock behavior. Back in seventh grade, I'd never participate when my asshole friends picked on kids, but I wouldn't stop it, either. I'd go on my way. By spring of eighth grade, I couldn't let a single injustice go. I hated bullies, maybe because I felt like the world—at least the U.S. Air Force—was bullying me? Maybe because I figured life is short and brutal and stupid and mean people make it worse? I don't know.

Anyway, early that Wednesday morning, I sat on my bike and watched as this new kid at school, Riley, got shouted down by the old man who was dropping him off. The man (I know now the jackass is his grandpa, an old fart named Hoover) was completely vicious. He called Riley a pig. Seriously. I locked my bike and watched Riley walk away from the car. I could tell he was crying, which just about killed me. Then I followed Riley into the building. I don't know what I was going to do. Ask if him he was okay or something? I didn't get a chance. Once inside, my old best friend, Landon Anderson, came around a corner and for no reason at all called Riley a fat bitch and shoved him into a wall of lockers. What a great start to the morning, huh?

I didn't even think. I just jumped into action, charged right up to Landon, reached and grabbed him by his throat, slammed him up against a locker.

"Leave him alone," I hissed.

"Dude. You're psycho," Landon wheezed. "You don't say a word to me for a month but now this shit?"

While I held Landon's throat, Riley ducked and ran. Very courageous.

The bell rang and Landon shoved me away. "I don't want to, but I will beat the shit out of you," Landon said.

I was exhausted after that, like a zombie. Too much adrenaline expended or something.

Then, in Earth Science, group work! Oh, did I hate that crap. I didn't want to talk. How the shit was I suppose to participate in a group? I watched all my old friends form a group and then the music kids formed theirs and the gamer nerds formed theirs and the cheerleader chicks (including Natalia Carron) formed theirs and that left the criminal papier mâché butt builders, Mouse and Mattheson, the bullied boy Riley, Wiz and me. I flat out couldn't believe it when Wiz chose to join Mouse and Mattheson. What, was I going to be stuck working with Riley, that weak-jawed butterball who let me face his bullies alone?

I surveyed the scene, sighed. I didn't like anyone, but Wiz seemed less bad than the rest. Mouse and Mattheson

I figured were complete idiots, but they weren't part of any stupid clique. I looked over at Riley, felt pity for the fool, then took aggressive action. "Hey, Ms. Farhaven?"

She was startled, like she couldn't believe I was talking (I get it, since I hadn't talked since before winter break). "Yes?" she asked.

"Do you think me and Riley could join Wiz over there?" I pointed directly at the papier mâché butt.

"No!" shouted Mouse. "Not Mr. Basketballs! We have our group!" Apparently Mouse hadn't noticed my social decline.

Ms. Farhaven said to me, "You'll have to put up with the other two, you understand."

"What are we, reprobates?" Mouse shouted.

"Reprobates?" Wiz said. "You know that word?"

"We are Team Champion!" Mattheson said.

"I can deal with them," I said to Ms. Farhaven. I turned to Riley. "I guess we're with them."

Riley stared into space, but he moved when I did. We picked up our stuff and slid over to join our new group. And yeah, Riley dropped a pen and then a folder and had to bend down to pick his crap up. Yeah, other students looked on and laughed. Yeah, Landon Anderson, that dick sack, whispered, "Fat ass and freak show join the carnies." Yeah, maybe I blushed a little, embarrassed about what I'd become. But you know what? Right there, right at that moment, the Strange Times team was formed! Historic!

Of course, none of us knew shit, yet. Wiz glared at me when I sat down, because jocks had treated him like crap and he figured I was one.

Mouse shook his head, said, "Why us?"

Mattheson, who apparently didn't even recognize me from being in the same classroom with him all year and didn't even know who I was, even though we'd been in the same school for three years running, said, "Hey! We're going to build a ghost ass volcano for the Science Project. Wiz says we can run a plastic tube out a hole in this butt and blast vinegar and baking soda out of it!"

"We are not doing that!" Mouse shouted. "Respect the ghost girl!"

"The what?" I asked. "We're going to build what?"

"A ghost butt volcano," Wiz mumbled. He pulled down his aviator goggles.

"That's stupid," I said.

"Why?" Mattheson asked.

Seriously, did I really need to explain why building a papier mâché ass was a dumb idea for science project? I stared at Mattheson for a moment, then said, "Can we just meet up tonight to make a better plan?" Eighth grade sucked. I definitely didn't want to flunk and repeat it.

The bell rang.

"Oceannaire Coffee? Like 6:30?" I asked.

I hadn't said that many words to anyone outside my family in months, but what was I supposed to do? It was group work.

Strange Times, though, right? That was us! And, even though we didn't know shit, the strange times would start unfolding that very night.

CHAPTER FOUR

I wish I would've enjoyed the bike ride over to the coffee shop more. Maybe hit some jumps or something, because I wouldn't get to ride my dad's old Redline Proline BMX bike ever again.

I locked the bike to the rack behind the Oceannaire. The shop was close enough to the middle school that lots of eighth graders went there to work on group projects.

Riley stood right behind me—like two feet behind me, silent. We'd met at school so I could show him the way to the shop. He didn't say a damn word the entire time we rode. Not one! I should've had some empathy, right? I didn't like talking to people, either. But I had no empathy. Something made me hate him. I know now he was basically in a catatonic state, okay? Not only had he been forced to move away from his parents to grandparents who were butt-wipes, he was also having very, very scary dreams. I should've felt bad for him.

No way.

Riley seemed like one weird-ass, thick through the gut, creeper. Also, he rode a stupid rusted-out beach cruiser that he didn't even lock, which was also stupid. I had a cable and a U-bolt to deal with, because my old-school Redline was pretty dope. After I got the lock job done I motioned for Silent Riley to follow, then walked to the front.

Right then Mouse and Mattheson tore into the lot on their skateboards. Mouse was all frothy.

"Keep your eyes open, dude, and your nose and your ears. We can't miss any signs if she's sending them," Mouse said. He skidded to a halt about ten feet in front of us. "We must be vigilant."

"And sly," Mattheson said.

"What are you talking about?" I asked. "Who's sending you signs?"

"Look who's here! It's Mr. Fuzzy and Fatty McFartsalot," Mouse said.

"Mr. Fuzzy?" I asked.

Then a Beemer sped into the parking lot. It squealed into a spot nearby. The back right-side door opened and Wiz stepped out. "No," he shouted into the car. "No. I need a ride. I can't walk! God!" He slammed the car door and the Beemer pealed back and out. "One hundred percent asshole!" Wiz shouted.

"Hi Wizzy!" Mouse cried.

Wiz barely looked at us. He lowered his goggles onto his eyes and headed for the door. "Hey," he mumbled going in.

Everybody entered before me. I stood out on the sidewalk for a moment. Two idiot name callers, a freaking mute, and a dude who can't look at another human being without wearing goggles? *Really good idea choosing these losers for your science team.* I shook my head, wondered how I'd gotten to be such a loser myself. Then I remembered Dad, how life was pointless. My heart sank in my chest, and I stumbled into the store. Two idiots, a mute, a goggled freak, and a fatherless boy who almost cries in public . . .

Five minutes later, we sat around a circular table in the corner of the shop, all silent. Riley sucked on a giant coffee shake called a Moocho Choco. Wiz didn't get a drink and didn't look at us at all. He played a game on his phone. Mouse and Mattheson punched each other under the table. I sipped my smoothie, waited. Nobody said anything for a long time, so even though I didn't want to speak, I spoke. "Okay. So, I guess we have to do a science project, huh? All together. As a group, which is dumb, but whatever."

The other dudes just stared at me.

"So," I said, "What do you think?"

Mouse leaned forward and said, "I think you shouldn't be talking, because clearly Wiz should be our leader, Mr. Fuzzy."

There was that Mr. Fuzzy crap again. I didn't understand. "Why do you keep calling me that?" I asked.

"Because you grew a fluffy little fuzzy mustache in like a day, dude. It's hilarious," Mattheson said.

It was true. That fuzzy fur popped out on my upper lip in a blink. I didn't know what to do about it. I didn't know how to shave. Again, fatherless boy. "Oh yeah," I said.

"Fuzz or no fuzz, Wiz is our leader, because he's a man of science."

"Fine. Tell us what to do Wiz," I said.

Wiz still didn't look up from his phone.

"Come on, Wiz, tell these dudes how it's going to go down," Mouse said.

Wiz looked up but didn't say anything.

"Wiz-nut-ski!" Mouse shouted. "You're our leader, bro. Come back to earth!"

"Me?" Wiz mumbled. "I made a suggestion at school but you didn't like it."

"I liked his idea," Mattheson said. "Papier mâché ass that blasts foam out of its a-hole. That's funny."

I shook my head. So stupid. We were definitely flunking if we did that. "Yeah. But funny isn't the goal for the science fair," I said. "Plus, how is a plaster ass science? You gotta know that's not science, Wiz."

"I'm not in this group for the science," Wiz said.

"It is science, you idiot, because the ass is the ass of a ghost," Mouse said.

"Yeah, dude," Mattheson said. "For real."

Suddenly Riley sat up straight. His eyes opened wide. "Real ghost?" he asked.

"Yeah, bro. A real live ghost," Mattheson said.

"Ergo, we are providing scientific proof that ghosts exist, because we have a copy of her real butt," Mouse said.

Wiz stared at me through his stupid goggles. A smile crept across his face. He nodded slightly and smirked. I knew what he was saying. "Welcome to our group, asshole." Thing is, while Wiz didn't believe in ghosts back in the day, I did. I already knew, factually, that ghosts not only exist, but manifest regularly. See, my dad was more than an Air Force pilot, he was also a serious amateur paranormal investigator. I've always been interested in that stuff, too. And, because of Dad, I'd seen things that made me believe.

I actually got a spark of energy. I sat up straight. "Uh . . . okay," I said. "Mouse. Explain why you think the ghost butt is real."

"Because she's a real girl, dude. A magical dead one," Mouse said. "Thus she's a ghost and thus she erased traffic on Highway 101 last night, and turned the moon red, and walked out of some fog, and she wants me bad and she's coming for me tonight at some point, so I might not even be part of this project, but you can still use her plaster ghost ass to blow out some foam. That is my gift to you."

"The moon? Red?" Riley asked. "Is she a blonde ghost girl?"

I turned to look at his face, which had gone totally pale. Something was going on with him, for sure.

Wiz startled everyone. He pretty much shouted, "What are you idiots talking about?"

"She's why I got hurt," Mattheson said, pointing at the Band-Aid on his head.

Pals, for the first time in a long time, I felt interested in shit that was happening in front of me. First, Riley, who had been a damn zombie, looked like he'd been slapped. The dude was suddenly fully engaged, totally terrified. Second, Wiz, who had been all mumbly before was suddenly pissed! He pulled his goggles off his head and said, "You're saying you got attacked by a ghost on Highway 101? That's what you're saying?"

"Sorta," Mattheson said.

"Not attacked, dude," Mouse said.

"But she touched you?" I asked. "She physically hit you? That's weird."

"Not touched. She smelled me and breathed on me, though," Mouse said.

"Was her breath cold?" I asked.

"Yes, bro! Totally! Like ice!"

Riley stood up. He hugged himself. I could see giant goosebumps rising on his arms. "You okay?" I asked.

He shook his head, said, "Uh-uh. Uh-uh. No," then sprinted, like top speed, right out the door.

"Whoa! Fast for a fat boy!" Mattheson said.

I turned back to Mouse, too curious to worry about Riley. "Was there a strange smell in the air?" I asked him.

"Like metal sort of," Mouse said.

"What in the world are you guys talking about? Why did that big boy just run away?" Wiz shouted.

"Yeah, metal," I said, nodding. "It's like an iron smell, right?"

"Exactly," Mouse said pointing at me. "I think."

Wiz turned his attention to me. "Are you supporting this delusion? Are you suggesting these idiots actually saw a ghost?"

"Yeah, sounds like it," I said.

"Oh my God. This is ridiculous," Wiz said. "This is exactly why I don't spend time with people my own age. You're all stupid."

"My dad isn't stupid. He tracks ghosts," I said. As soon as those words dropped out of my mouth the sickness enveloped me again. Dad told me never to talk about his investigations. I'd never mentioned it before to anyone. But there I was, saying it in front of these fools. Talking about Dad like he was just a regular guy who lived in my house like other dads.

"So your dad's a psycho?" Wiz said.

"No," I said. My eyes watered. My head hurt.

"But he believes in ghosts? Chases them?" Wiz said.

"Yes," I said, more quiet.

"So he's crazy, because he believes dead people's spirits walk around the earth. Does he believe in witches and sea monsters and space aliens, too?" Wiz asked.

"Shut up," I said.

"He does, doesn't he?"

"Shut up. Seriously," I said. Anger started to burn through the fog.

"Oh this is great. This will help me get into MIT, right? I joined a crack team! Thanks Dad! Here I am, hanging out with normal kids! A couple of idiots and the son of a psycho," Wiz spat.

Oh, that was too much, pals. I stood up so fast, the chair I was sitting on flipped over backward and slid across the floor. The whole coffee shop fell silent. Everybody stared. Especially this giant hippie-looking bearded dude. He leaned way forward, a fat hippie smile on his face. And my body trembled. My hands shook. I swallowed hard. Looked down at Wiz. "Don't you ever call my dad a psycho again," I hissed at him. "If you do, I will end you, do you understand?"

Wiz's face froze. Mouse and Mattheson stared up at me, mouths hanging open. I turned and bolted out of the shop.

CHAPTER FIVE

What a good first meeting, right? Two group members basically ran away. Strange Times wasn't off to the best start.

Let's begin with Riley. He ran away first. Seemingly for no reason. At least I had gotten in a little fight with Wiz, who was sincerely acting like an asshole, I believe. Riley just took off. Man, he was scared.

Remember when the ghost girl told Mouse she'd been showing up in his dreams? That wasn't true at all. I'm about a hundred percent sure Mouse had never dreamed about her.

Riley had, though. For months (maybe even longer, he now thinks), he'd been having intense dreams involving a blonde girl who looked like she was living in the 1970s, who got attacked in her bedroom, murdered by some vicious shadowy creature while the room shook and bookshelves collapsed and dust rose in tornadoes around her. She screamed, kicked, and cried, but couldn't stop the thing from destroying her. In his dream two nights before our Oceannaire meeting, Monday night, the girl's soul had separated from her writhing body and it had slid into a hole that opened next to her bed. Before disappearing, her soul had clutched at that splintering wood of her floor and looked up, straight into Riley's eyes (he'd never been part of the action before that). She'd cried, "Will you help me? You need to help me!" He said he would, but then he woke up and he sure as shit didn't want anything to do with this girl or this dream or ghosts or anything. Riley had enough trouble in his real life. Parents, grandparents, punk ass bullies . . .

Riley biked away from the Oceannaire on his stupid beach cruiser. The light changed. It was getting dark. Riley didn't know where he was going. He had no idea. He'd only lived in Encinitas for two months. He biked and biked and biked. In circles, around a big park, into neighborhoods that weren't familiar to him and then back out. He was totally lost. Scared as shit. These were seriously shitty times.

Poor Riley was really tired of being scared.

Riley hated his new life and his new house and his grandparents and all the crap Hoover pulled. For instance, Riley rode on that dumbass, broken down, rusted out beach cruiser because Hoover—who refused to be called grandpa or anything like it because the old man was an asshole— had sold Riley's fat tire mountain bike to, quote-unquote: "Help pay for the food you inhale every day, fatso."

Wrong! Riley knew for a fact that his parents gave Hoover money to cover Riley's expenses!

Hoover sold that bike just to be a dick, just to get money for more beer. What kind of grandpa does that? Sells his grandkid's prized possession?

Riley's back hurt on this stupid beach cruiser. He hated it. He hated Hoover. He hated every stupid asshole California kid, too (he told me this—other than me, Wiz, Mouse and Mattheson, he still doesn't love California kids). Damn he missed his Utah friends. Back when he lived there, he and his buddies listened to dope music and played sick video games. They sure as shit didn't get haunted! They didn't make ghost asses out of plaster! The year before, when they had a science project to do, they wrote a team report on how chemicals in water were making male frogs grow female parts. Those frogs were losing their wangs, pals. That's a good science topic!

Ghost butts? What the hell?

Riley rode and rode. Finally, by total accident, he ran into our middle school. From there he knew how to get home.

No way we should be messing with ghosts, Riley thought. He rolled down the road that would take him to Hoover and Memaw's apartment building.

Maybe Ms. Farhaven would let him do his own project? He could re-make the poster he and his buddies had made, showing a bunch of different kinds of frog mutations.

Dim streetlights lit the street in front of him. He got the chills. Creepy as hell.

Here's the truth: Riley is what ghosts call spongy. He is permeable. He naturally sees ghost energy, hears ghost thought. He had the specific dream about the blonde ghost girl getting murdered, but she wasn't the first. He'd been seeing ghosts, dreaming about ghosts, his entire life. He didn't need to study ghosts. He lived among them, and knew it, even though he denied it again and again during the day, while fully awake.

Riley ascended a small hill, pushing on the creaking cranks as hard as he could. And then, there it was: his building. His new home. Harbor Shores apartments, built for near-dead old folks who wanted nothing to do with kids. And yet, there he was, a kid living with his grandparents (freaking Hoover and Memaw), both of whom wanted nothing to do with kids, either. But they had no choice, did they?

Riley rolled down a small slope to the edge of the giant parking lot that surrounded Harbor Shores. Instead of crossing, Riley plunked down the cruiser and sat on a curb and stared up at the blackening sky. Only three months earlier, even though he had scary ghost dreams, he had been a happy kid. He'd always known his parents did something illegal to put food on the table, but it seemed stable. They got away with growing and selling for years, he told me. They were so settled in, when the bust came, his parents couldn't believe it. "What are you doing? Why are you doing this?" his mom shouted at the cops. It was like his parents just thought of themselves as normal small business people. But Riley knew better. He could never have his friends over. He lied about what his parents did for money. "Dad's an accountant!" His family had a secret life that came exploding out into the open.

And now his parents were serving jail sentences that would keep him away from home and his friends pretty much forever. His parents are still in jail now and will still be when Riley graduates from high school.

Riley stared up at the moon, which rose to the east, somewhere over the mountains out there. Riley missed seeing real mountains. When his mom told him he'd be moving to California to be with Hoover and Memaw, Riley thought he'd at least be on the beach, which sounded okay. But he hadn't gone to the beach once since moving to Encinitas. The only reason Riley knew the ocean was nearby was because he'd seen it when he went grocery shopping with Memaw one time.

The moon was totally huge.

The moon was scary, actually, because it reminded him of the end of the dream he'd had on Monday night. He told the blonde girl's soul he would help. She slid up out of the hole. He opened his mouth. A giant moon lit the sky overhead where there was once a roof. The girl's soul began to slide into him, into his mouth, but then the Shadow attacked. It blotted out the moon, shrieked and reached into Riley's mouth, down into his throat. It grabbed the girl's soul and tore it out of him. The girl screamed and cried the whole time. The Shadow's hand shredded Riley's esophagus. Blood poured into his stomach and lungs. The Shadow cried out, "That's your reward for being such a hero."

Goosebumps rose on Riley's arms again. He blinked hard. He looked around him. He stood, grabbed the bike, and rolled it quickly across the parking lot.

Riley could feel something close by, but he couldn't name it. He couldn't see it yet. He couldn't hear it yet. He couldn't smell it, but he could feel her. Riley broke into a jog.

In a tunnel just beneath Riley, just a few feet below the surface of the parking lot, the same girl from his dreams, the same girl who made traffic disappear around Mouse and Mattheson the night before, trailed Riley. She looked for an opening, for energy, for the opportunity to meet Riley, to slide into him and be safe.

Most ghosts are scared, just like Paula was.

Yeah, Paula was her name.

CHAPTER SIX

So that was Riley, right? He ran out of the Oceannaire because talk of the ghost scared the shit out of him. Dude didn't know there was no place for him to run, because Paula, who had physically located Riley, was just biding her time (she sucked on batteries and used energy being released in the Earth's crust to get stronger).

What about me? I ran out of the coffee shop because if I didn't, there was a good possibility I'd end up punching Wiz in his skinny little face (poor Wizzy probably would've broken in half back then; he's at least a little bigger, a little stronger now that we've all been together for a while). Damn I was pissed. How could that bony piece of crap, Wiz, act like such a dick to me? Just because he dressed like a little freak mad scientist didn't mean he knew anything at all. In fact, Wiz didn't know! I knew!

I'd seen stuff a nerd like Wiz could only read about in his nerd fantasy books!

I stomped around the side of the building. I kicked the wall of the shop while making my way (imagining Wiz's face). I couldn't wait to get on my dad's bike, couldn't wait to tear out of there, get away from all these assholes! That's what I felt like all the time back in eighth grade. *Where did all the assholes come from? So many damn assholes in the world! Why would I talk? Why would I even bother?* I turned the corner at the back of the building, to where Dad's bike should've been. But . . .

Bike? "Where is it?" I said out loud.

The slot in the rack where'd I locked the Redline was empty. Every muscle in my body filled with adrenaline. My eyes darted up and down the full bike rack. My chest got so tight.

Oh shit . . . Oh shit!

You know, I owned a perfectly good SE, a pretty sweet one that rode great. But, after Dad's disappearance, I started using his old Redline Proline all the time. It was a little bike, and it was heavy as shit compared to the SE, but it was also dope in a vintage way (white leather bar pads with silver snaps). Back in the summer before eighth grade, back when Dad was still acting like my dad, we'd clipped the Redline into a stand and Dad had taught me how to rebuild a bottom bracket. We put new cranks on the thing, too. It rolled smooth.

While Dad sprayed oil on the new chain, he'd said, "Man, when I was fourteen, I spent every cent I made doing a paper route on this bike. Your grandma wanted to beat me up—I was supposed to save for college."

"Turned out okay, right?" I said. "You got to college, anyway."

Dad pulled the brake lever, stopped the rear wheel from spinning. "Yeah, well, I had to go to a military academy to pay for school, buddy. Maybe I'd have a normal job now. Maybe I'd be an absent-minded professor or a scientist if I'd just saved that money, gone to a local college, instead of buying a rad bike, huh?"

"You wouldn't have met Mom if you didn't go to school in Colorado. I owe my life to you buying this rad bike," I said.

Dad laughed. "I guess you're right. This is a seriously important bike!"

It really was a seriously important bike. I rode it everywhere. Sometimes some of the hardcore BMX kids made fun of me because it was such an antique, but a few of them were BMX history nerds and they'd say things like, "That bike is old-school gangster, bro!"

Yeah. It was old-school gangster.

It was gone.

I sucked for air.

Oh shit . . . Oh shit . . .

Fifteen minutes? That's pretty much how long I'd been inside the shop. How could this happen? How could thieves break a Kryptonite lock and saw through a cable in fifteen minutes without anybody noticing? I mean, shit, it was still light out for the most part.

I didn't know what to do. I pulled my phone out to make a call, but just stared at the bastard, instead. I wanted to call Dad, but I couldn't call Dad. I didn't want to talk to anyone else. I pretty much fell down onto the curb and put my head in my hands and again, at the old age of fourteen, there I was crying in public. It's possible I would've run away that night. At least dropped out of school . . .

But a couple of minutes later, I looked up and there was Wiz, about ten feet from me, staring at me through his stupid goggles.

"What?" I asked.

"My mom and dad won't give me a ride home," he said. "They're out for dinner." He paused for a couple of seconds before saying, "Uh, why are you crying? It's not because I called your dad a psycho, is it? I . . . I didn't really mean that."

"I'm not crying. I have bad allergies or something," I said.

"Are you getting picked up?" he asked.

"No, I have to walk," I said.

Turns out, Wiz lives fairly close to me. My family doesn't have the kind of sick cash his parents have. He lives backed up against woods and shit. I live backed up against somebody else's backyard. But, still we're close.

"Oh good. Great. We can walk together," Wiz said.

"No. I want to be alone."

He lifted up his goggles. "Please, Charlie. It's getting dark."

"What? Are you scared of ghosts?" I asked.

"No," he said. "Rapists and murderers."

For some reason, that made me laugh. I stood up, said, "Let's go," and started the long walk home. I only turned back to look at the spot where my dad's good, old bike had been once. Shit, pals. Still makes me sick to my stomach.

Of course, I would see it again. Just not nearly in working order.

Wiz didn't say very much as we climbed the hill up towards the big ass Natural Trails Park that separated our school's neighborhood from where we lived further to the east. I know now what he was thinking, though: *Don't be a jerk. Be a cool dude. Be funny and charming, so Charlie Wilkins likes you. Charlie Wilkins is the kind of ass-face dick sack Dad will count as a "normal" friend . . .*

Yeah, thanks a lot, Wiz. That's really what my good friend used to think of me. Ass-faced dick sack.

We walked for a few minutes, then I got jumpy. "Where are Mouse and Mattheson?" I asked. I looked over my shoulder and turned right, onto a side street. Wiz followed.

"They took off," Wiz said. "As soon as you were out the door. I guess they think they can find their ridiculous ghost girl . . . no offense intended, Charlie. I'm not saying all ghosts are ridiculous, just theirs."

"None taken," I mumbled. I looked over my shoulder again. There was no doubt in my mind. An alarm in my head was going off. We were being watched.

"They want to get ghost molested, so they went to find her," Wiz said. He stopped walking suddenly. "You're not really heading to the trails, are you?" he asked.

"What? I don't know. Keep walking." By that point, I wasn't paying much attention to Wiz at all. I had gone into a subdivision that backed up against the trails, true. Why? I had a bad vibe. A big, bad, bearded, fat man, hippie vibe.

Five minutes earlier, about three blocks from the Oceannaire, I had seen the same big hippie who had been watching us, a little too intently if you ask me, while we all got in the fight at the coffee shop. He stood behind a Jeep and stared as Wiz and I walked up the sidewalk across the street from him. I didn't think anything of it then. But, a moment earlier, when I felt like we were being watched, I turned and saw the same dude behind the same Jeep parked across the street from where Wiz and I were walking again. I got very nervous.

"It's getting pretty dark," Wiz said. "I know there aren't a lot of pedophiles and killers around here, but it only takes one, you know? Wouldn't want to get unlucky cutting across on a deserted trail when we could just take ten or fifteen minutes longer and stay on the street."

"Yeah. I don't know. I think we're being followed," I said.

Wiz stopped again. "Are you messing with me?" He had been wearing his goggles on his forehead since the Oceannaire. He pulled them down on his eyes. "Because it's not funny at all."

I took a couple of fast steps and crouched behind a Toyota. "Come here," I said. "Did you see the hippie? That big old fat dude at the coffee shop?"

Wiz's shoulders crept up to his ears. He nodded. "Beard," he said.

"Yeah. Seriously. Come here," I said.

Wiz moved and crouched next to me. Not more than five seconds later, a Jeep came round the corner. It skidded to a halt. The hippie pulled himself up using the front roll bar. He seemed to sniff the air.

"Pedophile?" Wiz whispered.

"What is he sniffing for?" I asked.

The hippie's head swiveled in our direction. Wiz and I ducked fast.

"Where the heck you think you're heading to, Charlie Wilkins?" called a gravelly voice. "You're not going to cut up through them trails and over across Olivenhain, are ya?"

"He's talking to you," Wiz whispered.

"Yeah no shit, Wiz," I said. "Okay. Okay. I'm going to talk to him." My heart pounded in my chest.

Wiz put his hand on my shoulder, pulled down. "Don't do it," he said.

"I have to. What if he has my dad's bike?"

"What?" Wiz asked.

I stood up, my shoulders and head clearing the top of the Toyota. "Okay . . . Okay, dude. Did you take the bike?"

"No, I sure didn't. I got no bike."

"Shit. Fine. Why are you following us?" I shouted.

"Uh, to make sure you get home okay?" the hippie said. "You got a lot of company, right?"

"Company? Yeah. You!"

"Ha ha. I know you're your dad's kid. I know you got the sixth sense, right? You can feel them shadows and shreds traveling the sewer lines, can't you?"

"What the hell is he talking about? What the hell?" Wiz gasped.

"Go away or I'll call the cops, man," I said, holding up my phone.

"No need for that, little dude!"

"I'm calling 911 right now!" I shouted. "Pedophile on the prowl!" I took several steps up the hill, onto a stubby cul-de-sac where the Natural Trails area connects to city streets. "Let's go, Wiz," I said. "That fat ass won't be able to deal with the trails."

"Listen," the man said, holding up his hands. "If you go up in there, he's going to scare you, okay? Tunnels open to the surface in there. But . . . but he doesn't have much power for real. On a normal day, he can make a lot of noise, but as long as you stay away from the cottage itself, he can't hurt you. So, just be cool, got it? Don't freak and run off a cliff or nothing."

"What is he talking about, Charlie?" Wiz asked, standing straight up, revealing himself from behind the Toyota.

"Hi buddy! You must be part of the team, huh?" the man asked Wiz.

"Team?" Wiz said.

"Just go away!" I shouted. "Come on," I said to Wiz. Then I turned and began to jog into the growing dark, to the trails.

"Wait, little dudes. Just come back here," the man shouted.

"Stick it in your ass!" I cried over my shoulder.

"Yeah!" Wiz shouted. "All the way in!"

"Ha ha! Will do!" shouted the man. "Hey! Charlie! When you get home, look for that book! The guest book, okay? You know that book? We need it! Hey . . . hey! Why don't you just come back here?" the man cried.

But we were cruising away up into the Natural Trails Park.

"What book? Guest book?" Wiz asked.

"I don't know what the hell," I said.

We didn't have much time to wonder about the hippie dude, though, or his weird ass questions, or what the hell he meant when he said, "He's going to scare you . . ."

CHAPTER SEVEN

We climbed into the hills. The damn terrain was tough to deal with. Wiz was not remotely stoked about the situation. We ducked low-hanging branches and we tripped over dips and holes in the ground. We both jacked on the flashlight on our phones, which allowed us to see a little bit ahead, but not much. It was getting dark, very fast.

Wiz stopped at the base of a small rise. "Why are we in here?" he spat. "I don't even know what direction we're going in. The compass on my phone is all messed up. It's like we're going through electromagnetic fields, or something."

"We're fine. I've been through here a lot. I think . . . I think I know where we're going. Just keep walking," I said.

"Oh good. Great. I'm really feeling better about this," Wiz said.

Then, as we scrambled up a scrubby hill, navigating all these jagged rocks, both our phones, for no apparent reason, buzzed like we were getting texts.

"That's weird," I said.

"Yeah," Wiz said. He leaned over onto a large boulder next to a sharp-tined bush to the trail's left. The boulder seriously looked like a skull—two giant eye sockets, anyway. "Really. Did you get a message?"

"No," I said, staring at the boulder. Then my phone shocked me, like literally zapped my hand! "Ow," I shouted.

"This is very strange," Wiz whispered. He held up his phone. It sprayed an arc of sparks from its charging port, which bounced off the skull boulder.

"Jesus! Ouch!" I got shocked again. I dropped my phone into tall, sharp grass. The flashlight went out all together. Then Wiz's phone went dark, too.

"Something entirely odd is going on," Wiz said. His voice cracked.

I nodded. Tried to catch my breath. Not that Wiz could've seen me nod, because the darkness around us intensified. I mean it was freaking blackness! This is not how it tends to get dark in Encinitas, either. We get some really good, long sunsets. I reached down into the grass, trying to find where I dropped my phone.

"No snakes, please. No snakes, please. No snakes," I whispered, pretty sure I was a moment away from grabbing a rattler, getting bit, probably dying, and so I wasn't particularly aware of the temperature dropping steadily. But Wiz was.

"Hey. It's getting really cold. Like . . . like ice."

I found my phone. Pressed the on button. For a moment, the light shined into my face. I could see my breath, in Encinitas, in late spring! I turned to look at Wiz, who stood behind me, illuminated by my phone. "I don't think this is good," I whispered. Then my phone turned itself off.

"No," Wiz whispered into the dark.

"Yes. It's really cold here," said a child's voice.

"Did you say that?" Wiz asked.

"No," I said.

"So cold," said the child's voice.

"Oh no. Oh shit, Charlie," Wiz mumbled into the dark.

I couldn't see anything, or I might've run away. I was seriously about to shit my pants. I could tell Wiz was in the same boat.

"You don't want to be here, Charlie Wilkins," the kid's voice said. It was closer.

"It knows your name," Wiz whispered.

"No, I really don't want to be here," I said, throat closing with fear. "Go away, kid, or whatever you are . . ."

"You're the sixth generation, not the fifth. You don't have to be here," the voice said, even closer.

"Dope!" I shouted. "I'll go!"

The thing, the voice, spoke again, "Paula is the fifth. Leave her be and you are safe."

I could feel the ice of the kid's breath on my neck and that was it. Even though I couldn't see shit, I grabbed Wiz's arm and yanked. "It's on me, bro! It's on me!" Then I took off, pulling Wiz along.

The thing, the kid voice stayed with me. "If you save Paula, you will take her place!" it cried in my ear.

I smacked at my face with my left hand, trying to smash the thing like a bug (it didn't have a body!) and pulled Wiz with my right (he was screaming like in a horror movie). We sprinted into total darkness, up over a hill and then into an opening where there were fewer trees.

"This is a cemetery!" Wiz cried.

We skidded to a halt. "Maybe we lost it?" I said.

Then a shimmering light appeared in front of us. A glowing boy's face, so pale white it was translucent, with deep-set black eyes, a tall forehead beneath, like, an old-time paperboy's cap, and a pointy nose and small, blackened, rotting lips.

"Ah!" I screamed. We both ran the opposite direction, up a rise. Somewhere there my foot caught on a rock and I fell hard onto my chest, sliding across gravelly soil. The boy was on me immediately. "Stay away from Paula of the fifth," it whispered in my ear. "Or you will take her place and you will be so cold."

"Get away from me!" I screamed. I rolled over onto my ass and crab-walked backwards.

"Stay away from Paula," the child's voice said. "Stay away, Charlie Wilkins. Stay away, away, away, or . . ."

Over the rise from the other direction came a set of headlights.

"A car!" Wiz cried. "It's a real car!" Actually, the lights were attached to a Jeep that bounced over rocks and quickly closed in on our position. "The hippie!" Wiz cried.

It came so fast Wiz had to jump out of the way and I had to roll. The Jeep slid to a stop.

"Back off, Rooster!" the hippie shouted. "Charlie and nerd kid, get in here!"

The hippie didn't have to ask twice. Wiz was in the passenger seat before "nerd kid" slid out of his fat beard. I leapt up into the open vehicle a tenth of a second later. The hippie smacked the gas and we took off, bouncing down the gravel access road we must've been on when I fell on my chest. I was so shocked, I barely registered what was happening (including the blood seeping out of my shirt).

Suddenly a wicked wind blew from the right. It pelted me and Wiz with gravel.

"Uh oh. Little boy's pissed!" said the driver. "We're close to his energy source. This is going to look worse than it actually is!"

The hippie accelerated and the Jeep bounced hard. I flew up and hit the top of my head on the roll bar.

"You okay?" Wiz shouted.

"I don't know," I said.

"Hang on, little dudes!" the hippie cried.

He floored it and the Jeep roared into a dip then bounced out on the other side, catching air. Wiz and I hung on for our lives (I held the bottom of the seat with my right hand and gripped Wiz with my left).

At that moment, a line of scraggly pine trees to the right burst into flame. One by one, they uprooted and flew into the Jeep's fender.

"Holy shit!" I screamed.

"This is not happening!" Wiz screamed.

"Whoa-ho-ho!" the hippie shouted. "We got fireworks!"

We spun off the road to the left, totally crushed through a row of bushes then skidded back onto the road.

"We're almost out!" said the driver.

Thank baby Jesus for that! My face was already peeling off from screaming. But it wasn't over. The child's face materialized, white as a sheet in front of me. It hovered calmly. Its black eyes were open wide, like a damn zombie. "Stay away from Paula, Charlie Wilkins," it hissed. "Or you will die!"

I'm not shitting. I howled and cried and slapped at the thing. Wiz screamed and cried and slapped, too. The child's face smiled, then disappeared. The Jeep bounced over a curb and out onto the normal streets of Encinitas.

"Oh my God. Holy shit. Holy balls," Wiz said.

"I didn't think you should go in there, little dudes. But the ghoulies never come out this far. They can't. We're safe now!" Just then we hit a pothole in the road and Wiz bounced up and smacked his goggled head on the roll bar. He slid down on the seat and stared straight forward.

"Whoops!" said the hippie. "Safe from the ghoulies, anyway!"

"Safe?" I shouted. "Who are you? What the hell is going on? Who was that thing? That kid? Why'd he know my name?"

"I'm Cortez, dude! Figured you might want a lift out of there, once you got in and met Rooster."

"Rooster?" I shouted.

"The fugly dead kid!" Cortez said.

Fugly for real. Man. I could only nod at that. I put my hand on my chest and felt the sticky blood on my t-shirt.

"You're bloody," Wiz said, nodding.

"I'm going to get you two home," Cortez said.

I looked back over my shoulder. I couldn't see any fire reflecting in the night sky. I couldn't see smoke hovering over the Natural Trails or the old cemetery (which is called Olivenhain Cemetery we were soon to find out). Were the flying trees real? Was the fire real? Was any goddamn thing real?

Cortez squealed around a corner in the general direction of my house. He tore up the street. A minute or two later he pulled the Jeep over.

"What are we doing?" I asked.

"Doing?" Cortez asked.

"I'm going to get out," I said.

"Sure, little dude. I wouldn't trust me. I mean, look at me. Ha ha ha!" he said.

"You're wearing a Mexican poncho," Wiz mumbled.

"You got that right," Cortez said. "Anyhoo, here's the deal. You listen to me. You trust me, okay? You don't have much time. Are you listening, Charlie Wilkins?"

I was, but I guess I looked stunned or something. I looked the hippie in the eyes. I nodded.

"Good. Listen real good. By dawn Saturday, this whole deal will be done. If you want to save her, you're going to need to get me that book. You know the one I'm talking about, Charlie?"

I shook my head, no.

"It's a guest book thing? From down at the Whaley House? You know about that house? Historical and what-not? Packed to the gills with the ghoulies?"

I shook my head, no, again, even though I had heard of the Whaley House from Dad.

"That damn book is mine and I'd go in your house and get it myself, but I can't see through your old man's bird cloak, even though he's gone . . ."

"What? My old man's cloak?" I asked.

"Yup! Your dad! Me and him are buddies, right? So he told me about that cloak—some kind of bird squawking thing? And how I can't get inside, so I need you to help me by finding that book, by getting me that book. Get me that book and I'll help you save the girl."

"What girl?" Wiz asked.

"I don't know any girl," I said.

"If you don't yet, you soon will," Cortez said.

Then I thought for a second. "No. No way. Can't help with the book. Sorry." I knew my dad well enough. If he built some cloak or whatever that kept this dude away, there was a good reason.

Wiz grabbed my wrist. He gripped tight. "Aw, really? Come on, Charlie," Wiz said in a very weird, slow way. "I mean maybe you can't get him the book tonight. But tomorrow? Or Friday? Jeez. We can trust him. He just saved us, right?"

I squinted at Wiz. He was turned away from Cortez. He lifted up his goggles and winked at me.

"Oh. Yeah. That's what I meant. Just not tonight," I said.

"Not tonight. No problem! We still got tomorrow and Friday!" Cortez said. "Get it to me by Friday midnight and we'll beat Yankee and that kid, you and me! We'll save the girl and save you!"

"You bet we will," Wiz said.

"You bet," I said, nodding. Yankee? That was the first I'd ever heard of who we now know is Yankee Jim Robinson. Just hearing *Yankee* back then sent a chill up my spine. I didn't know why.

"So you got to get a hold of me, right? Cell phones don't work with all them ghoulies." Cortez leaned way forward, pretty much across Wiz's lap. He opened up the glove compartment and pulled out a pair of old army walkie-talkies. He handed one to me. "Here. You know how to work one of these?"

"Yeah," I said. Dad had some in the garage, so I actually did know.

"You can get a hold of me on this. Analog, so rock solid in a pinch," Cortez said. He was still leaning across Wiz.

Wiz tapped him on the shoulder. Cortez sat up.

Wiz spoke like a robot. "That's fantastic. Charlie will get that book by Friday night. Drop us off at my place: 2307 La Noria."

Cortez nodded. He smiled. "Right on, little dude. You're a good one, aren't yuh?"

"Uh huh," Wiz said.

Cortez nodded again then hit the gas and the Jeep leapt forward. Again, I held on both to the seat and to Wiz, so

I wouldn't fly the hell out. The walkie-talkie bounced in my lap. A few minutes later we rolled down a wide street bounded by large glass houses. Wiz's street.

"Right here," Wiz said.

Cortez skidded to a stop and we climbed out.

Cortez said, "Listen, Charlie Wilkins. I'm a good guy. Like a white hat cowboy guy, okay? The nerd boy gets it, right?"

"Yes, sir," Wiz said in his robot voice.

Cortez turned back to me. "Your dad was balls deep in this stuff for years, but it's just beginning for you, so get your head on straight. It's Wednesday, so Saturday morning is coming, right? Just over two days."

"Did you say my dad *was* balls deep?" I asked.

"I did. And he was," Cortez said.

"Right. Saturday morning. Two days," I mumbled. I thought *Dad was* . . .

"So don't dilly dally," he said. "Get the book and we're gold. Don't get the book and either she's a goner or you are, got it?"

I nodded. "Me or her."

Cortez smiled big. "If you need some help or want a chat, give me a honk on that walkie-talkie."

I held up the walkie-talkie and nodded.

"See you real soon!" And with that, the hippie Cortez took off into the night.

Wiz turned and began walking up the street fast, away from the house where we'd been dropped off.

"Where are you going?" I shouted after him.

"You think I'd give that psycho my real address?" Wiz shouted without turning back to me. "Now, go away, Charlie Wilkins. I don't know why, but you and your fat hippie pal just spent tens of thousands of dollars trying to scare me with all your crazy special effects! Oh yeah, take the nerd into the cemetery! Project ghost boys on bikes! Now, stay away from me!" Wiz began running.

"Ghost boys on bikes?" I shouted. "What bike?"

Wiz didn't answer. He ran.

That made *me* mad! I mean, why was the nerd upset with me? It didn't make any sense. We both got the shit scared out of us and *I* was specifically threatened, right? Plus, how the hell would I have created a giant special effects extravaganza for him up there on the trails? Fiery trees shot out of the ground at us! I didn't even know we'd be up there after our meeting!

"You're a jerk!" I shouted after him.

He turned to his right and ran into the woods surrounding a giant glass house.

CHAPTER EIGHT

I couldn't go to school Thursday.

First, I was mad at Wiz and didn't want to look at his nerd face.

Second, I was so tweaked by Rooster the ghost boy, I didn't sleep all night. Any time my eyes closed for more than a few seconds, his bony, white face and deep black eyes appeared in my mind and I shook awake. What was all that crap about *Paula of the fifth*? Did he say I was the sixth generation? *What the hell?*

Third, I kept sweating, thinking, *what the hell did that fat-ass hippie mean when he said it would all be over on Saturday? What would be over? Am I going to be over? Ghost boy said I would die if what? I saved her? Who? Paula? Holy shit!*

Fourth, the hippie (Cortez) gave me that damn walkie-talkie and there was no off switch. It made weird noises periodically. Once it said, "Get the book." Once, at around 3 a.m., it seemed to say my name a few times . . . *Charlie* . . . *Charlie* . . . *Charlie* . . . (I buried it in the closet after that).

Fifth, my damn body just hurt. The scrapes on my chest from falling on the gravel were pretty wicked and my head ached and my wrists, too (I guess from catching myself when I fell).

By morning, I was completely wrecked. School? No possible way.

Thankfully, my mom is a nurse and she took one look at me and decided I wasn't making my illness up (no, I didn't show her the scrapes on my chest—Mom had enough stress in her life: no husband, three kids, etc., I didn't want to add "son involved in ghost violence" to the list). My big sister Lindsey figured I was faking, though. She gave me the finger over the breakfast table, before she left for school.

Then I went back to bed and had bad dreams about ghosts and hippies and Wiz. Meanwhile, my little brother Dez made a shit-ton of noise all morning, which kept me jumping out of bed, because with each crash of a toy or little boy shout, I figured I was getting attacked. Dez was barely a toddler at the time, so I didn't blame him for being a damn lunatic, but he was definitely driving me crazy, like out of my mind . . .

Things didn't get quiet in the house until around two in the afternoon, when my mom took Dez to his daycare and she went for her shift at the hospital. Then I slept heavy, pals. Dreamless and pain free. Until four, anyway, when I heard shouting outside the house, which again made me think I was being attacked by a little boy ghost.

I shouted, cried out, jumped from my bed, peeled back my shade and looked out the window.

There were boys outside the house. They just weren't little dead ones and they weren't named Rooster. They were three dipshits named Wiz, Mouse and Mattheson (no Riley, please take note. Also, I love them like brothers, now—I'm a dipshit, too).

I didn't exactly want to see them, and I was still pissed at Wiz for running away like he did, but for some reason I was kind of glad they were there. I walked to the front door and opened it. "Hey. What do you want?" I asked.

Wiz was lying on the front yard. Mouse and Mattheson stood on their skateboards, leaning over him. Mattheson turned to me. "Hello, Mr. Fuzzy. Did you know Wizzicles doesn't know how to ride a skateboard? He doesn't ride a bike, either. He's like a little baby, with no wheels."

"I'm not a baby," Wiz muttered from the ground. He'd clearly run a long way, probably all the way from school, trying to keep up with Mouse and Mattheson on their boards.

"Fuzzy!" Mouse shouted. "You're wearing your Batman PJ's, aren't you? That's pretty dope, man. I wish I had a pair."

I looked down at my legs. Yeah. I was wearing Batman PJ's. "Uh, shit," I said.

"Can we come in?" Wiz asked, still on the ground.

"Aren't you all mad at me?" I asked.

He rolled up to standing. He shrugged. He lifted his giant backpack onto his shoulders and walked towards me. Mouse and Mattheson followed.

"Okay, I guess you can come in, then," I said.

As soon as he was inside, Mattheson asked for food. I gave him some old tortilla chips. He liked them. Mouse asked for something to drink. I let him look in the refrigerator. He immediately downed two of my mom's Diet Cokes, which she doesn't let us drink.

Wiz was all business, though. His cheeks were hollowed out. Even through his goggles (yes, he wore them almost all the time back then, the freak show), I could tell his eyes were red. "You couldn't have been responsible for the ghostly special effects show," he said. "You didn't know we were going to walk together."

"I know," I said. "I wouldn't know how to do that, anyway."

"That fat hippie must've rigged it all up," Wiz said.

"I don't think anything was faked. We saw a ghost," I said.

"No we didn't. Ghosts don't exist," Wiz said.

"Yes they do," Mattheson said, mouth filled with chips.

"I want to go back to the Natural Trails to look for evidence of the fakery," Wiz said. "I want you guys all to come with, because we're a science team and I want to prove once and for all that men of science don't believe in ghosts!"

Mouse let out a huge Coke burp that pretty much shook the house. "How about instead we stay here and watch a little TV."

Wiz turned to Mouse. "Please come with me? Please let me prove that somebody, probably a fat hippie, is messing with us?" Wiz turned to me and Mattheson. "Please guys?"

"How can you prove that, though?" I asked.

"It was a big sound and light show. The hippie had to have left some traces of that behind," Wiz said.

I shook my head. I really didn't want to go back there.

"Please!" Wiz said.

What was I supposed to do? Wiz was really desperate (he didn't tell me until later that he dreamt that Riley was dead and a girl lived inside his dead body, which really shook him up, apparently). "Fine. Okay," I said.

"Yes!" Wiz shouted.

Then out of no place, Mouse said, "Hey. Is your dad around? He investigates ghosts, right bro? Maybe he can help us."

My gut clenched up hard. "Dad. Dad is gone. With the Air Force."

Silence hung in the air. They all stared at me. I think my chin trembled. Something tipped them off, anyway. Mattheson reached over and slapped my shoulder. "Bro," he almost whispered. "Remember your PJ pants? Batman doesn't cry. Batman kicks ass when he's sad or scared, right?"

I looked at him for a moment. Mattheson didn't know me at all (he didn't even know I was in his science class just a day before). But, it was like the dude somehow *knew* me. "Yeah. Batman does kick ass," I said. "Let's go."

CHAPTER NINE

I changed into legit out-of-the-house clothes, then went to the garage and grabbed my SE. On the street, Mouse and Mattheson were doing ollies and crap.

"New bike? Where's your old-school gangster Redline?" Mouse asked.

How many punches in the gut can one young boy take? "Uh, I lost that bike," I said.

"I saw you on it yesterday," Mouse said. "Are you totally lying, bro?"

"No. Seriously. It's gone," I said. "Wiz, I'll double you up."

Wiz sighed, then climbed on my seat. He put his bony hands on my hips. Rolling like that was awkward. But what were we supposed to do, make Wiz run after us? We set out for the Natural Trails.

"What the hell are you carrying in that backpack?" I shouted, pedaling hard. "It has to weigh a ton!"

"I really count on having my stuff. You never know when a specific tool or book will come in handy," Wiz said.

What a damn nerd. It was so hard to keep us rolling. That ugly slogging made Mouse and Mattheson very happy, though.

"That bike ain't built fer two nerds!" Mouse cried. "We gotta knock one off!"

While I stood and pumped the shit out of the pedals just to keep up momentum, Mouse and Mattheson repeatedly cut close in front of us, which made me hit the freaking brakes, which made Wiz cry out in pain ("You're killing my testicles!"), which made Mouse and Mattheson laugh and keep the shit up.

"You dudes are such idiots," I shouted, but they kind of made me laugh, too, which felt pretty good.

"Least we know how to ride a bike!" Mattheson cried.

Although it took far longer than it should have, we eventually made it down the hill from my house to the El Camino Real entrance to the Natural Trails. Now, I hadn't asked the dudes if they'd invited Riley to come along, but I'd wondered about him. I was aware that he wasn't with us. And so, I was sort of relieved to see Riley when we got to Natural Trails. I figured Wiz had told him where to meet up with us, which apparently wasn't the case. He'd actually just shown up.

"Oh shit, you're alive!" Wiz cried. (Again, he hadn't told us yet about the dream of dead Riley he had the night before.)

"I am?" Riley asked. "That's good."

"How did you know we'd be here?" Wiz asked.

"Wait, you didn't tell him?" I asked.

"Where are we?" Riley said.

Pals, Riley looked sick as shit. "What's up with you, bro?" Mattheson asked.

"You weren't in Ms. Farhaven's class, dude," Mouse said.

Riley shook his head fast. "Wait. Wait. Why are you boys here? I don't like it here. This is a bad place. Tunnels and shreds, Charlie Wilkins. Enemies!" These confusing words were by far the longest utterance that had ever fallen from his mouth.

"We have to be here. We're doing some investigating," I said.

"Did you see the special effects last night?" Wiz asked. "Is that why you're scared? I'm going to prove it was all fake."

"If I run, they'll take you, Charlie Wilkins. I don't want them to get you!" Riley shouted.

Yes, dude freaked me out. My heart began to pound. "Just come with us. Just relax," I said. To show I was relaxed, I locked my bike to a wood fence post (although I knew locking a bike wouldn't necessarily keep it safe). Then I said, "Okay, Wiz. Take us to the place where we saw the ghost boy last night. I honestly couldn't tell you where we were."

"*Fake* ghost boy." Wiz said. "I'll try."

"Ghost boy?" Riley shouted. "He's up there!" Riley pointed up the trailhead. "Right now!"

"Now?" I said.

Riley leaned towards me and growled. "Now. Now. Now."

"Riley?"

"Now!" Riley shouted. Then he stumbled over a bush, somersaulted like a rolling sausage, popped right back up to standing, pulled his shit beach cruiser off the ground and started running with it. He jumped to get on the bike, skidded to the side, hit a parked car, then turned back to me and screamed, "How can you keep us safe if you go right to where the boy is? How can you save me?"

"Stop! Come back here, Riley," I said.

The rest of the crew stood in stunned silence.

Riley kicked off the ground and pedaled away so fast. His acceleration was truly beastly. He turned and screamed again, then flipped us the bird.

"Something's very seriously wrong with that dude," Mattheson said.

"I don't know what to do," I said, watching Riley's figure recede down the road.

Wiz bent down and pulled his goggles out of his backpack. He put them on, lifted up his bag and began the trek up to the trails. "We don't have time for him. We have to find evidence before it gets dark."

"Yeah. Okay," I said. After that display from Riley, I was less than excited about heading back into the hills. Still, we followed Wiz onto the trail.

CHAPTER TEN

T he going wasn't easy even in the light of day. The path was steep, and grasses and tree roots seemed to reach for our legs. And soon, the path that had been in front of us sort of disappeared. "This is it, remember?" Wiz said to me.

I nodded, but I didn't know.

We climbed rocks and jumped down into sharp, ugly looking grasses (all I could think: *no snakes, no snakes, no snakes*).

"Are you sure this is right, Wizzy?" Mouse asked.

Wiz stood straight, looked around. "I'm not sure. But, I think so," Wiz replied. "It feels right."

And then, I saw it: a bush with sharp tines next to a boulder that looked less like a skull than I remembered, but still seemed to have eye sockets. "Wiz. Check out the rock. It started right by here," I said.

"Yes," Wiz nodded. "I fell into that bush. That's how I cut my hands up."

"You fell?" I asked. I didn't remember.

"Ow, dude!" Mattheson said. "I skateboarded right into one of those bitches one time. I had to pull prickers out of my sack for like days!"

Wiz looked around. "Yeah, this is the right area. Our phones got messed up by this rock and the boy rose from the ground right around . . ." Wiz spun. He blinked. "I'm not sure where the projection—the hologram or whatever—surfaced, exactly."

"What are we looking for?" I asked.

"A generator or . . . or a projector or even some matted grass where the projector or generator might've sat. Lighting rigs?" Wiz said.

"I don't see anything, bro," Mouse said.

"Well, except rocks and shit," Mattheson said.

"We need to cover ground methodically," Wiz said.

We stood and stared for a moment, silent. Then something clicked in my mind. Truth is, I'd watched my dad do investigations before. I had a pretty decent idea of what to do. "Okay. Here's the deal," I said. "I'm going to step off fifty steps toward the palm by the big rock over there." I pointed at a scrawny, dried up tree next to a rock. "Mattheson, I want you to follow me and step forty steps. Wiz, you step off thirty, and Mouse, twenty. Then we're going to walk a circle around the spiky bush and the skull rock . . ."

"Skull?" Mattheson asked.

"Yeah. Look at the eye sockets. See?"

Mattheson looked at the rock where Wiz had leaned the night before. "Oh yeah, bro."

"Yeah. So, we'll circle. All of us keeping as close to the same distance between us as possible, and we're going to look for clues—plastic, metal, prints where maybe somebody put something really heavy. After we go around twice, we'll comb through the interior of the circle. It's not foolproof, but this way we'll at least get eyes on the ground within a fifty-foot radius. Make sense?"

Mattheson raised his hand.

"What?" I asked.

Mattheson scrunched up his face. "Shit. I totally had a question, dude."

"Let me know if you remember it," I said.

"Oh, Fuzzy! Yeah! Shouldn't somebody take notes about what we're doing so we can write this up in the science report?" Mattheson asked.

Mouse's mouth dropped open. "Mattheson made a sound point, right? I mean, he's totally right, isn't he? We can use this investigation for the goddamn science project!"

Wiz nodded. "I didn't even think about it," he said.

"Sweet, man," I said to Mattheson, who looked very proud.

"After we get done with our investigation, I'll write up the particulars in my notebook," Wiz said.

Then I stepped off fifty approximately foot-long paces. Mattheson, Wiz, and Mouse all followed suit, stepping off the number of paces they'd been assigned. They began to circle, slowly, crashing through tall grass and over rocks. "Look for anything that seems out of place up here," I shouted.

In the first quarter of the circle we found plenty of shit that shouldn't have been in the park. Hot Cheetos bags, long ago fired bottle rockets, more used condoms than seemed humanly possible ("Who the hell is getting so much sex? Not me!" Mouse shouted). Mattheson found a dead black bird. Wiz found a Sony CD Walkman with an old Smiths disc in it. Mouse found more condoms ("What the hell?"). Then, in the second quadrant, Mattheson tripped on something and fell.

"Ouch, bitch!" he cried.

We all stopped walking and turned toward him. "What did you get?" I called to him.

"Some metal thing," Mattheson shouted.

"A generator? A projector or something?" Wiz called.

"No. Looks like an old bike wheel," Mattheson said.

A chill flew up my spine. "What kind of bike wheel?" I shouted.

"I don't know. BMX rim. Broken spokes and shit."

"Can you pull it out?" I asked.

Mattheson reached into the tall grass and gripped the wheel. He pulled as hard as he could, but the thing didn't budge at all. "No, bro," he said. "We'd need a shovel or something. It's pretty buried."

"Do you have anything you can use to mark the spot, so we don't lose it?" Wiz asked.

Mattheson dug into the pockets of his jeans. He pulled out a half-sucked red and white candy, unwrapped. "I got a mint!" he shouted.

"Tie your shirt on the wheel, dude," Mouse said.

Mattheson pulled off his t-shirt and tied it to the wheel.

Then we continued around the circle, searching. I kept my eyes peeled the best I could, but I was pretty seriously distracted. More than distracted. My mind spun. *Just because it's a BMX wheel doesn't mean it's your BMX wheel. There are like ten billion BMX bikes in Southern California. It's not yours . . .* But my heart pounded hard in my chest, because what if it was my wheel? What if that Rooster shit lord was the one who stole it from me? I just had a feeling. . . .

We completed our first circle a few minutes later. We found nothing else of interest, definitely no generators, projectors or matted grass caused by heavy lighting rigs.

"Should we go around again?" Wiz asked.

"Let's just think for a second," I said.

The four of us gathered back at the spiky bush. Mouse and Mattheson climbed up on the skull rock.

"Well, we found at least ten thousand used condoms. That means ten thousand girls are actually doing it in the world. That's so dope," Mouse said.

"No, actually it means ten thousand dudes are doing it," Mattheson said. "Girls don't wear rubbers, man."

"Yeah, dude, but the dudes have to be doing it with somebody," Mouse said.

"Your mom," Mattheson whispered.

"Ohh, shut up, bro," Mouse said.

"Yeah, please, shut up," I said. My stomach was burning. A dull pain began to throb behind my eyes. I knew what that broken, half-buried BMX bike was. Somehow, I just did. "Uh, I don't suppose any of you have a shovel on you?" I asked.

"Ha. Right," Mouse said. "Usually I carry around my trusty spade, but not today, dude."

"I have an archaeology trowel in my backpack," Wiz said. "It's not very big, but the blade is sharp. It digs pretty well."

"You are a nerd," Mouse said. "For real."

I tried to act normal, tried to hold my shit together. "Hey, you guys. Mouse and . . ." I looked at Mattheson, but couldn't even come up with his name. "You."

"Me?" Mattheson asked.

"Do a sweep of the twenty feet right around the bush, okay? See if you turn up some non-condom evidence. Wiz, grab your trowel. Let's see if that bike wheel means anything."

"You think it has something to do with special effects?" Wiz asked.

"I don't know," I said.

It took a couple of minutes, but Wiz found the trowel in his giant backpack. Then we made our way to the spot Mattheson had marked with his shirt.

The bike wheel was covered in a thick weave of bush and grass. Easy to see how poor Mattheson had tripped on it. I bent down and used Wiz's trowel to cut away the tangle. Just doing that work revealed about a third of a black rim surrounded by a flat street tire, held together by spokes that were mostly broken. The black rim was too familiar. "Jesus Christ," I said.

"What?" Wiz asked. "Special effects gear?"

I could hear how much Wiz wanted to logic all this shit out in his voice. There was nothing logical about what I was seeing though. "Let's keep cutting this crap."

Once we had removed as much of the bramble-y shit as possible, I got down on my knees and began digging into the dirt around the wheel. I jammed the trowel into the ground and hit something spongy. I dug around the spongyness and uncovered a dry, seemingly ancient, white leather cross bar pad. Right then I totally lost my breath for a moment. I dug a bit more and was able to pull the pad from the ground. I handed it to Wiz.

"Okay?" Wiz said, turning the pad over in his hands. "Wonder what this *RL* stands for?"

"Redline," I said, looking up. "Old-school BMX logo."

Then I really went to work. With each cut of the trowel, I became more sure of what I was seeing, what I was feeling. I was able to cut half way around the wheel (I found no more pads), but still couldn't get the wheel out of the damn ground. It took at least ten minutes to get this far and my hands were beginning to blister. Mouse and Mattheson finished the second part of the search and were screaming in the background. They kept hitting each other with large, dead palm fronds. Man, they irritated me so bad, but I didn't stop to tell them to shut the shit up. I knew this wheel was my dad's wheel and I knew the crossbar pad was from my dad's bike so I just went at the digging, hard.

"You okay, Charlie?" Wiz asked. "You look a little . . . uh, crazed?"

"There's some chrome down there, right? You see that shit?" I asked.

"Chrome?"

"Like a bike fork. It's attached on one side. Here. I'm going to try to pull this whole thing out."

"Okay?" Wiz said. "Wait. What's that?"

"What?" I asked.

"That . . . chain. It's not part of a bike. It's . . . holy balls?" Wiz fell down on his knees next to me. "Is that a watch? Or a compass?" He dug into the dirt with his hands and pulled out what appeared to be an antique pocket watch. "I . . . I own something like this. I mean, really, exactly like this. I was looking for it last night, because . . ."

"Oh. That's interesting," I said, as if I was even remotely interested in the watch. I threw down the trowel and squatted over the wheel. I grabbed the rim and began to pull on it as hard as I could. I felt it slip a bit in the earth, so I doubled my effort and let out a long, "Gahhhhh!" Blood began to seep through the front of my shirt. "Wiz. Help me pull on this thing, man," I shouted, heaving for air. "I have to get this thing out of the goddamn ground, okay?"

Wiz stuck the watch in his pocket then wrapped his arms around me and pulled, too.

"It's moving!" I screamed. "Keep pulling on me!"

And then, the bike wheel (and a partially attached chrome fork) came out of the earth with a pop, lightning quick, so fast that we flipped over backwards.

"Ahhh!" Wiz cried.

"Oh shit. Oh shit. Are you okay?" I said. "Did I hit you?"

Mouse and Mattheson leapt through the bramble and over rocks to get to us. They pulled Wiz to sitting. Slowly he lowered his arms from his face. The left lens of his aviator goggle was cracked in a spider web pattern.

"Bro, that fork almost took out your damn eyeball," Mouse said.

"Baby Jesus," Mattheson said. "Now I know why you wear those things!" He immediately pulled his shirt back on. Maybe for protection?

Wiz, still stunned, reached up and removed the goggles from his face. He stared at the broken lens. "You could've brained me, Charlie," he said. "Probably make my dad happy."

"What?" I asked.

"Hey," Mattheson said. "There's more shit in that hole you made." Mattheson leaned over the spot where the bike wheel had been removed. "Is that a shirt?" He reached down and pulled not a shirt, but a pair of extremely dirty, child-sized Incredible Hulk underpants out of the hole. "I have these! They're my favorites ever! I ate a whole pizza in third grade wearing undies like these and nothing else! I caught our dog one summer right before he ran out in the street in front of dump truck. I was wearing these damn undies! They're the best! They don't fit on my body anymore, but I keep them for good luck!" Mattheson turned them around in his hands. "Hey! Check this out! They have my initials on the tag just like my mom put my initials on the tag of my hulk undies!"

"Dude, those really are your initials," Mouse said, seeming confused.

"Yeah!" Mattheson said. "And I wrote a big M for Mattheson in sharpie on the left ass cheek . . ." Mattheson's face suddenly pinched up. He looked at us. He rotated the undies outward so we could see their ass side. A big faded M was scrawled there. "What in the shit is going on here? These are my Hulk undies! How the hell'd they get in this hole?"

Wiz dangled an old-time train conductor's watch in front of us. Its back was ripped off and the gears were smashed. "This was in the hole, too. My gramps got it for me for my tenth birthday. My initials are engraved in the cover. After my goggles, this watch is . . . was my favorite possession."

Mouse fell on his knees and dug in the hole. He pulled out a Han Solo action figure that was missing an arm and a leg. "This belong to one of you?"

It didn't. Mouse jammed it into the pocket of his jeans then went back to digging. We all watched, quiet and scared as shit. "My Globes!" Mouse screamed. "My brother got this shit in like 1999, but never wore them and gave them to me!" He pulled a cut up, dirt covered gray and orange right shoe from the ground. "Oh dude, no! Totally gangster Globes just got killed in this dirty shit sack hole!"

"I'd be willing to bet the Han Solo is Riley's," I said.

Wiz took a deep breath. "Someone got into our houses and stole our things and got back here and buried it all right where the special effects thing happened last night," Wiz said, quiet as can be. I don't think he was buying the special effects explanation anymore. He looked up at me. "But they didn't steal anything of yours?"

"No, they did," I said. I still held the bike wheel in my hand. I lifted it up and everyone stared. "My dad bought this bike in 1983. He spent all his paper route money on it."

"Oh dude. That's worth even more than my undies," Mattheson said.

Suddenly a cold wind picked up around us. A piece of paper slowly rose from the hole. It rode the air and spun up in front of us.

"Ghost boy?" I said. "Are you here?"

Nobody and nothing answered me. The paper just danced in front of us. Mouse reached out and grabbed it. The paper was old, wrinkled, dirty. Words were scrawled in black, or maybe burnt, across one side. Mouse read the words then turned the paper to us.

BICHES U SAV HER I TAK EVER THING

"What the hell does 'sav her' mean?" Mouse cried.

"Save her," Wiz said. "The boy. The . . . the projection from last night told us not to save a girl. Her. What was her name, Charlie?"

"Paula," I said.

We all stared at each other for a few seconds.

"Who the hell is Paula?" Mouse asked.

I shrugged.

"Riley wants Charlie to save him, too," Mattheson said. "Remember?"

Riley had asked how I was going to save him right after he hit that parked car on his bike.

"I have to see my gramps," Wiz said. He reached down and grabbed his trowel from the hole and marched away.

"Right now?" I shouted after him.

He didn't even turn back to us. "Yes!" he shouted.

I took a breath. I wasn't sure what I should do for a second. Then I remembered the live walkie-talkie buried in my closet. I remembered the hippie's request. I turned to Mouse and Mattheson and said, "My mom's not home. You two dudes want to help me find a guest book?"

They both looked pretty stumped by that one. Didn't matter that I confused them though. Mouse and Mattheson will go along with just about anything. They're so damn cool. And, the dudes helped me carry the pieces of my dad's dead Redline out of Natural Trails Park and to my house where we got to work looking for the book.

CHAPTER ELEVEN

I think we better address Riley. He pulled some stuff, some crazy stuff, while the rest of us were slowly becoming a team.

Genevieve Francis, then fifteen years of age, reported via Twitter that she saw a very fat kid bunny hopping a beat-to-shit beach cruiser on top of picnic tables at Orpheus Park. "Like magic," she wrote. "He could jump on a car if he wanted to." There was a very Riley-looking, but blurry, picture attached to the Tweet.

Hy Luong, owner of the Circle R Minimart, reported to police (including Natalia Carron's cop dad), that a blonde and portly young fellow ran into his store, smashed a rack of discount romance DVDs with a head butt then ransacked a Little Debbie display, making off with over three dollars in Swiss Rolls. The police failed to pursue the matter, but Natalia accused Riley of being the boy on the old-school security videotape her dad had shown her the following week (for some reason the two digital security cameras in the store had malfunctioned). Riley said, "That wasn't me. I was with these guys!" He pointed at me and Wiz. Truth is, he wasn't with us. He remembers stealing several Little Debbie Swiss Rolls.

Finally, Perry Brown, who played the bass drum in the Union High School Pep Band at the time, updated his Facebook status to say: *Attacked by Fat Boy! He used my drum like trampoline! He jumped onto roof of my house! Dad shot him with a BB Gun!* The status was shared several hundred times. Everybody thought it was a joke.

It wasn't a joke.

The following day, Friday, I saw a BB-like wound on the back of Riley's neck.

You saw how he behaved at the park entrance, too. You can probably figure it out.

The dude was literally not himself.

CHAPTER TWELVE

Anyway.

The next day I asked Wiz why he took off from the park like that, abandoned me, Mouse and Mattheson.

Answer? Wiz was terrified. He ran all the way home.

His understanding of the world, of reality itself, had taken a serious hit. Until he found his own gold watch in that hole, he was convinced everything we'd seen the night before had been faked. But how had something (someone or some being) gotten into his house, into his secret treasure box, which was in a false bottomed drawer that he had built, that no one else even knew about? How had somebody stolen that watch and gotten it back to the park and buried it in a hole with a bunch of other stuff stolen from multiple other locations? There was no particularly

80

plausible explanation. And the best explanation totally sucked! It had to be . . . paranormal?

The dude was utterly exhausted by the time he reached the palatial house his parents built (before Strange Times, Wiz didn't engage in much physical activity). There was no time for rest, though.

Because the whole building is essentially made of glass, Wiz could climb on the bed of his gramps' pickup and see that his parents were sitting in the dining room, eating dinner. He figured that was good, because they wouldn't be looking for him. Wiz climbed out of the back of the truck and ducked into nearby bushes to keep out of sight. If his mom saw him, she'd make him come in and eat and she'd ask all kinds of questions about how his day was and if he had much homework (crap that clearly didn't matter given the shit he'd just witnessed). He had to stay hidden.

At the corner of the house, he slid out from behind the bushes and darted. It was pretty damn dark back there, so chances of him being sighted by his parents were slim, but he still moved like a ninja. He dipped into the backyard, which was built into the side of a wooded hill. He climbed up a path through scrubby pine. Lights glowed between trees up ahead. Classic rock vibrated in the air (apparently Gramps plays that shit often). The noise and lights came from the shack where his gramps did his thing.

Wiz grabbed a windowsill and stood on his tiptoes so he could see in one of the windows. Hope you can picture this as well as I can, pals, because it's good shit.

Inside, Gramps, wearing a welders' mask, held a torch to the bottom side of an old riding lawn mower. A record spun on the portable stereo in the corner. Jimi Hendrix shredded, which caused Gramps to bob his head while he burned metal.

Gramps makes Wiz happy in about a hundred different ways. The way the big old dude sort of danced when he worked on his inventions was one of them. Yeah, there was something seriously funny about an old man, a big-bellied fellow in a welder's mask, doing a little head-bang to wicked guitar. If our boy Wizard hadn't been so weirded out by what had happened in the park, by what we'd all unburied, he might've laughed. Instead, he stared at good old Gramps and breathed, trying to calm down.

Gramps, a former green beret, knew when he was being watched. He looked up, shut down his torch, pulled up his mask and started screaming, "God dang it, Wizard, you do not stare at a welding torch unless you're wearing your God dang goggles. You want to go blind?"

Wiz hung his head and walked around to the open front door and then in. "How did you even know I was out there?" Wiz asked.

"Felt your beady eyes on my flesh, boy," Gramps said. "Where you been? I could've used a second pair of hands a couple hours back."

"Sorry. I have a science project for school I'm working on. Group stuff."

Gramps squinted at him. "Are you lying to me? This is a real group with real members who I could call and speak to?"

"Why would I lie?"

"You're not sneaking around town, smoking the wacky tobacky?"

"The what?" Wiz asked.

"Doing the hooch? Partying with Mary Jane?"

"What are you talking about?" Wiz said.

"Snuffing crack?"

"Crack? No. I'm doing a science project in a group with four other people because it's a requirement for school, okay?"

"Uh huh. Sounds dumb," Gramps said. "Put on your goggles. I got to make this weld, kid."

Wiz slid his pack off his back and pulled out the goggles and put them on. He wasn't sure how to talk about the subject he wanted to talk about, so he tried to act like things were normal. Gramps, who didn't notice the spider web of cracks in one of Wiz's lenses, pulled down his own mask, and went about his business, attaching what looked to be extra blades to the under carriage of the Wisniewski's lawn mower (which wasn't the same mower Gramps was building into a helicopter that Mouse would eventually crash). When Gramps was done with the weld, he pulled up his mask, put down the torch and examined his work.

"That new blade is as sharp as a machete. I could mow through the jungle."

"Okay," Wiz said.

"You have something on your mind?" Gramps asked. "Normally you'd get excited about a lawn mower that could mow the jungle."

Wiz took a deep breath. He nodded then said, "Yeah. Okay. This is a little ridiculous, I know, but I have my reasons for asking. Do you believe in ghosts, Gramps?"

Gramps looked up from the mower. "Why the hell would you ask that?"

"Because. I've seen some stuff," Wiz said.

"Nothing you should be messing with," Gramps said.

"I don't want to be!" Wiz said. "I don't believe in ghosts . . . I mean, I don't want to believe in them. Are you saying you do?"

Without even a pause, Gramps responded, "Yes, I do."

"Don't screw with me old man," Wiz said. "I really can't take it right now."

"Nobody's screwing. I saw souls leave the bodies of soldiers over in Nam. Sometimes they went up, sometimes they wandered off, sometimes they came right for you. I bet there are ghosts here in these woods now."

Wiz pulled the goggles off his face. "Are you seriously serious?"

"Dead," Gramps said.

Wiz shook his head. "Okay. So . . . why didn't you tell me this before?"

"I'm not in the business of scaring wussy kids to death."

"Ha ha," Wiz said.

"Who's laughing?" Gramps asked.

"Oh," Wiz said.

"Help me get this mower outside," Gramps said.

I've met Wiz's dickhead dad. How Gramps ever let that jerk marry his only daughter, I'll never know, pals. Anyway,

Wiz grew up half under the sway of that jerk, who made Wiz feel like a total fool for reading fantasy books, who wouldn't allow for anything amazing or magic or whatever in the world. But then Wiz saw that odd stuff himself, and when Gramps confirmed Wiz's suspicions about the world, shit changed for the dude. He didn't need any more proof that ghosts exist. He needed to learn everything he could about them. He wanted to protect himself. He wanted to catch one. He wanted to save the girl. He wanted to protect me. Wiz wanted to know goddamn everything.

(Have I mentioned how much I like the dude?)

While Wiz helped Gramps roll the mower out from inside the shop, he asked, "Hey, Gramps, do you know of any devices that could repel ghosts or at least detect them when they're nearby?"

"Maybe," Gramps said.

"Maybe?" Wiz asked.

"Maybe I haven't used any of that sort of material in the last few decades, but when you've killed as many men as I did back when I served this country, you learn how to protect yourself from phantoms in the night."

"You've had to fight ghosts?" Wiz asked.

Gramps pushed the mower under a lean-to connected to the side of the shop. "I have not," Gramps said. "But I know how to."

"How?" Wiz asked.

"You track them down with a Mel Meter or a Gauss Meter. You pop them into dust with a reverse engineered cattle prod. Get a Springer Magrath Stock Shock. Reverse it. Instead of zapping, it sucks a jolt of energy. Ghosts disintegrate without energy. Old Springer Magrath sucks them stupid."

"Can you help me make one of those?" Wiz asked.

Gramps crossed his arms and leaned over him. "What the hell are you into, kid? Don't give me any more bullshit about group work and school, either. I know you better than that."

"This is for my group," Wiz said. "From school. I'm serious."

Wiz really was.

CHAPTER THIRTEEN

When I invited Mouse and Mattheson back to my place, I'd totally forgotten one thing: Thursday night was my night to read books to my little brother. It was my night to get him ready for bed. Weird I forgot, because reading to Dez was one of the few things I actually enjoyed at the time. Mouse, Mattheson and I rolled up in front of my house. It was beginning to get dark. I saw Dez's head in the kitchen window, staring out into the side yard.

"Oh shit. My little brother . . . I have some things I've got to do before we can look for the book. Can you guys wait out here for a little bit?"

"No," Mattheson said.

"What?" I asked.

"We don't wait for nobody," Mouse said.

He handed me the Redline's crossbar pad. Mattheson gave me a part of the crank we found in the hole.

"Okay," I said. "Sorry, but I have to get my little brother ready for bed or my mom will have a breakdown tomorrow. I guess I can look for the book by myself." Pals, I didn't want to look by myself. But what was I supposed to do?

I tapped the code into the garage and then rolled my SE in. I dropped the broken pieces of my dad's old bike in a big milk crate where we kept baseballs, softballs, and a flat volleyball. When I came back out to the driveway, Mouse and Mattheson were waiting. "You didn't go away," I said.

"We don't know what to do," Mouse said. "So we're standing here, bro."

There's something you should know about Mouse and Mattheson. Before that science project in eighth grade they were like a nation unto themselves. Since all the way back when Mattheson moved in next door to Mouse in preschool they'd spent all their time together, day and night, all weekends, all summers. Even though Mouse had a bunch of older brothers, even though Mattheson spent a lot of time watching Netflix with his mom—was dedicated to her huge—these dudes' main family was each other. They developed habits and rituals and shit. One of their "family" policies was that they would wait for no one (whatever the hell that means) and yet, there they were, standing next to their skateboards on my driveway, Mouse holding his ripped up Globes shoe, Mattheson holding his torn and grungy little boy Hulk underpants.

"We don't wait for nobody, dude," Mouse said again.

"But we want to stay here, okay? Because we want to help. We just aren't waiting for you, but we'll be here anyway," Mattheson said.

Yeah, that made no sense. "Okay," I said.

They both looked really serious, also sort of sad, and maybe a little scared—we had just dug their shoes and underpants out of something that seemed like a grave, right? I didn't want to do it, but I didn't think I had a choice given the forlorn expressions on their faces. I invited them inside to (not) wait, which was a risk, because my sister Lindsey was home, and she would likely see them, and she would likely tell mom I'd joined some kind of freak show. "Come on in," I said. "You can eat more of those chips, Mattheson."

"Dope, bro," Mattheson said.

Lindsey seemed to be in her room, which was good. Dez was waiting for me. Mouse, for no apparent reason, slapped Dez a high-five, which made Dez happy. Mattheson ate some chips and Dez and I went back to his room.

As we were walking back there I thought, *Where the hell is that Cortez book? A guest book from the Whaley House? Is it really in here someplace?*

It took a long time for Dez to fall asleep. Unfortunately, seeing Mouse and Mattheson sort of jacked him up and he rolled around a bunch the first few times I read through his favorite book, *Skippyjon Jones*. He asked to see my friends. He asked for water. He wanted to hear the book again.

"Again!" Dez shouted. "Again!"

"Seriously, dude?" I asked.

Dez nodded.

But while I was reading *Skippy* for the ninetieth time, getting all dry-mouthed and headachy, El Blimpo, the big fat Bumble Bee in the book, suddenly reminded me of Cortez in his striped poncho, and at that very moment I had what can only be called a vision. It was of my dad hunched over the desk in his office, paging through a weird, old, leather bound photo album. It was the night before he left on the mission he wouldn't return from. He'd been so sad at dinner, and I was totally scared and worried and I couldn't sleep, so late that night I climbed out of bed and wandered into the hall, and there was a light coming from Dad's office because the door was cracked open. I stood there in the hall and watched Dad stare at this book and scribble notes, then turn a page and stare again. I watched for maybe four or five minutes. Dad suddenly turned around. His face went completely red, his eyes burned. "Get out of here! Go!" he shouted. I ran back into my room. His shouts woke up Dez. Dez cried and cried. Dad and Mom got in a bad fight. In the morning he was gone.

Yeah, that's the last memory I have of Dad. I remembered his face and his yelling at me again and again. I didn't ever think about the book.

That book. That photo album thing. A guest book?

Thank baby Jesus Dez fell asleep during that reading. I tucked him in and tip-toed out of his room, down the hall past Dad's closed office, and into the living room.

Matheson's eyes were wide. Mouse's mouth hung open. "Is something wrong?" I asked.

"Bro," Mouse said, "Your sister . . . she came out here for a glass of water. She . . . she is the sickest."

"The hottest girl ever in the world, dude. Why didn't you tell us?" Mattheson asked.

"Shut up," I said. It has become a growing issue ever since. All the dudes in the Strange Times crew get completely stupid around Lindsey. What can I do? I just try to keep them away.

"She went to her bedroom," Mouse said with sincere reverence.

"Seriously. Shut up about her. Follow me," I said. "Quietly."

I tiptoed back down the hall. Mouse and Mattheson followed. They were quiet. The dudes are naturally sneaky, so they're good at this kind of thing. We entered Dad's office. Once all three of us were in, I shut the door and turned on the light. I hadn't gone into the office since Dad disappeared. It made me too sad. Mom and Lindsey never went in, either. For some reason, I think they'd have been pissed to know I was in there. Leaving the office like he left it just seemed right. I took a deep breath.

"Did we pass by your sister's bedroom?" Mattheson asked.

Mouse looked around at the shelves filled with books and the photos of UFOs and Bigfoot and the Loch Ness monster on the wall. He stared really closely at Bigfoot. "This is a dope room," Mouse said.

Then Mattheson looked around, too. He also got right up close to Bigfoot and squinted at the shot. "Yeah. Monstery as shit. You can almost smell that Sasquatch, it looks so real. Where'd you get all these pictures? Are they from movies?"

"My dad took them. They're all real," I said. They are too. We didn't have a lot of time to get this job done, though, so I couldn't get into it with them. "Listen, my mom gets home before eleven on Thursdays. We have to move fast," I said. "You guys look in that closet, okay?" I pointed at a set of accordion doors on one wall.

"Okay," Mattheson said. He pulled open the doors. "Looks good. Lots of shit."

"Are we looking for something inside that closet, Mr. Fuzz?" Mouse asked.

"A big brown guest book. Like leather cover. I think it might help us figure out stuff about the ghost girl," I said.

"Awesome." Mouse saluted and both disappeared into the closet.

While they were in there, I sorted through everything in the giant metal desk, pulling files from drawers, ripping through all the papers and crap in them (lots of weird stuff, but not a leather book), feeling for trapdoors underneath the desk, because Dad was definitely capable of building weird stuff like that.

In fact, the only reason I know Dad actually investigated crap like this came from something weird he built. I went into Dad's office in seventh grade because I was looking for my Christmas presents (I knew I was probably getting a football signed by Phillip Rivers, which is something I really wanted at the time). In the closet, I found this big, two-ball, bowling ball bag, which seemed like a good place to hide the football. So, I opened it up, but there weren't any gift footballs or even bowling balls in there. Instead, I found a bunch of wood slots that held these fat folders labeled "RESTRICTED ACCESS" on one side of the bag. On the other side, there were little leather boxes. I opened a couple of the boxes and found weird crystalline rocks and baggies full of dirt samples and little manila envelopes filled with shredded fabrics. I also found two black and white comp notebooks (like Wiz carries) filled with notes and sketches Dad had made.

The entries were about UFOs and hauntings and extra-terrestrial monsters. I really couldn't believe it. Why would Dad spend time tracking scary bullshit when reality was so scary already? Dad was sent all over the world on Air Force missions that were dangerous—to Iraq, to Afghanistan. That year, he'd spent a couple months away, moving between Turkey and Saudi Arabia. Why would he spend his free-time chasing Bigfoot and shit? Seemed dumb.

So, I hauled that bag out and dropped it in Dad's lap on the couch.

At first, Dad was pretty pissed at me. "Jesus, Charlie! You are not to go into my office, do you understand?"

But I didn't back down. I accused Dad of playing with toys like a little kid instead of being a parent. (He had failed to shoot hoops with me that morning, so I was already sort of mad.)

"Okay, okay," Dad had said, holding his hands up. "So you really care what I'm doing?"

"Yeah, because it seems really stupid," I said.

"The mysteries of life are stupid?"

"If they're just, like, stories drunk people make up, they're stupid," I said.

Dad laughed. "Most of what I research does turn out to be the product of a paranoid imagination, true. But, there are times when I get to see the real deal, kid, and it is so important to the future of this world, and I do my part to document it and to keep it safe."

"What do you mean safe?" I asked.

"Hard to explain. How about this? One of these days, I'll let you file a bowling ball bag report for yourself, okay? We'll discuss what it all means then."

Dad was true to his word. I did get to file a report. A couple of months later, Dad woke me up before dawn and I followed him into the garage. As the sun began to color the sky orange, we drove the Jeep down to the beach. Dad drove right out into the sand, which seemed crazy.

After he parked, he pulled out this old looking leather case, which had an actual film camera in it. He plugged a black, plastic cartridge into the camera and then aimed it out to the ocean. I know why he used real film now instead of digital shit (paranormal entities often zap out digital equipment), but I didn't then.

"Charlie. Grab the mic and the boom box. We'll try to get some sound, too, okay?"

The boom box recorded directly to cassette.

Just at that moment, a freaking crazy, giant spout of water fired out from the surface of the ocean. It had to be less than a hundred feet from where we were.

"Hey hey hey!" Dad cried. "Amazing, right?"

"Baby Jesus!" I shouted.

The thing jumped high into the air then fell backwards, almost like a killer whale at Sea World. It was a damn monster! It was part dinosaur and part fish!

"Alien species," Dad said. "That thing doesn't belong on earth."

"Whoa. I can't wait to tell my friends," I said.

Dad put his hand on my shoulder. "Oh, no, Buddy. Can't do that. We're not doing this to show off. We're doing this to keep humans safe, do you understand?"

"Okay," I said.

Honestly, I didn't really understand, but I didn't tell anyone either. Things were changing, though. Mouse and Mattheson were digging through my dad's shit in his closet. And Dad was long gone.

It took Mouse and Mattheson about twenty minutes to determine there wasn't anything in that closet that resembled a guest book (they did a great damn job crushing a bunch of cardboard boxes, which Mom pretty much kicked my ass for later). I couldn't find the book in Dad's desk, either. I was surprised. If it was in my house, seemed likely that we'd have found the book in Dad's office.

"Now what, bro?" Mouse asked.

"I don't know. Maybe you guys should go home. I don't think it's here."

Mattheson folded his arms over his chest and leaned back. "No way, dude."

"You won't leave?" I asked.

"I bet it's here," Mattheson said. "Where is he? Can you call your dad and ask for clues?"

Pals, would that not have made my life better in so many ways? "No. That's not going to happen," I said.

"Is there some little place in this house your dad would put something important and secret because he'd know nobody would look there, because the place is too gross or something?" Mouse asked.

At first I thought maybe I should go get the walk-ie-talkie and ask Cortez if he knew where it might be, because, other than his office, I couldn't think where Dad would hide something important. But then it was like I got slapped from inside my brain. Here's the thought that flew through my head at that moment: *Oh shit. Maybe in the crawl space? Balls!!! CRAP!!!*

I really, really hate that dirty crawl space, but it totally met the criteria Mouse laid out: too gross or something.

Freaking Dad probably stuck the guest book in the crawl space, because he knows how much that shit scares me, and he doesn't want me involved in his hobby any more, and he knows I poke around shit and maybe would've found the damn thing so . . .

"Let me go get my headlamp," I said. I turned and walked out of the room. I got an REI headlamp for Christmas a couple of years before. I don't like closed spaces too much, so I'd really only used that lamp for reading under the covers when my parents would make me go to bed way too early without my phone or anything to entertain me.

I wore the headlamp and went back into the room.

"Are we going into a cave, bro?" Mouse asked. He was holding my dad's Tony Gwynn signed baseball.

"Hey put that shit down, dude!" I shouted.

"What?" He put the ball down, though.

"Just follow me."

I tiptoed past Lindsey's room and then we headed out the front door and walked to the back of the house. I pointed at the two-foot-wide cellar window, the entry to the crawl space.

"Oh yeah. Crawl spaces suck, dude," Mouse said.

"I like them," Mattheson said. "Cozy."

"I don't like them," I said. I took a deep breath, mumbled *you're okay, you're okay, you're okay,* then pulled open the window and entered the crawl space. I flipped the light switch and two dull bulbs lit up, casting ugly yellow light. Mattheson dropped in behind me. Mouse, I guess, figured it was better to be the look out.

Once the two of us were inside, we were pretty much negotiating a three-foot-tall spider cave full of air-conditioning equipment, old boxes, and old luggage, which contained clothes Mom kept telling Lindsey would come back in style one day. Pals, I tried not to think about it, but I couldn't help thinking, *Spiders . . . Spiders . . . Spiders.*

"This place is messy as shit," Mattheson said. "My mom wouldn't let our crawl space get so disorganized."

"Well good for your mom," I barked. Dude was insulting my mom, wasn't he?

But yeah, to Mattheson's point, there was a lot of crap down there to sort through. Some of the boxes were too heavy for us to lift and move, so we had to brace our backs against the wall and shove them across the floor with our legs and at one point, while doing the shove, a spider—or some other crawly animal—dropped into the back of my damn shirt and I totally freaked and jumped up and smacked my head on the low ceiling (on the same spot I hit in Cortez's Jeep the day before!) and then fell forward, which caused me to overturn a set of file drawers that contained, among other things, my parents' stupid tax records from before even Lindsey was born.

"Whoa. That was epic, bro," Mattheson said, staring down at me (I was all sprawled out on the floor).

"Everything cool?" Mouse called from the window. "Nobody's out here. All's good in the driveway. Everything's under control!"

"Great," I said.

The files were all mixed on the floor and so I had to sort that shit out. It took me like fifteen minutes. While I was doing it, Mattheson dug through the boxes in the back of the crawl space. Oh, the dude was unhappy and the work was hard and dusty. Mattheson kept mumbling about how his mom wouldn't let important paper get so spidery and dirty.

As I got the last file put back together, Mattheson said, "There's not dick down here. Not anything but your putrid family papers, molding like fruit in the garbage."

I aimed my REI headlamp at Mattheson. "That sounded kind of like poetry," I said.

"Really?" Mattheson asked. He smiled big.

Then Mouse started shouting. "Car in driveway! Car, bros. Right now!"

Mattheson had clearly been in situations where he had to escape fast. Without even a word, he'd slid past me in the crawl space and had shot out into the backyard. Mouse must've taken off with him.

It was Mom's car. Of course. It came to a stop a few feet from the entryway to the crawl space. I knew she wouldn't be pleased to find me awake, digging under the house, way past the time I should've been in bed on a damn school night.

Hey, if Mattheson's mom is so neat and organized how come he wasn't worried about not being home on a school night? That's a good question, right?

Anyway, I flipped off the light switch then sat cross-legged on the cement floor, perfectly still, hoping Mom didn't notice the dudes running through the yard or that the window to the crawl space was wide open. Problem was, pals, I forgot to turn off my headlamp, probably because I was concussed from smacking my head on the ceiling! Anyway, I'm sure that little light under the house scared the crap out of Mom. I'm sure she didn't think, "My dumbass kid is crawling around under the house at midnight." I'm sure she thought, "There's a gang of prowlers stealing crap out from under our house!"

That's why she called 911.

I didn't know she called 911. I figured I'd stay put under the house for a while, wait until she was probably in bed, then I'd sneak in (I had my keys in my pocket so I could maybe get in unnoticed even though she'd definitely lock the door). But, fact is, she had seen Mouse and Mattheson run and she had seen my stupid REI headlamp lit up in the crawl space and so she didn't go to bed. She called 911, then went into her walk-in closet and pulled out the handgun she kept locked in her antique bureau, grabbed Dad's magnum flashlight and came back out to say hi . . .

I had relaxed a little and was pushing boxes back into place best I could (they were heavy as shit, though). Mom crept around the corner of the house and shined the light into the crawl space. It landed right on my face.

I shouted, "Oh shit!"

She shouted, "Charlie?"

I spun around and tried to file myself out of sight behind a filing cabinet.

She shouted, "Get your butt back out here where I can see you."

I knew I'd been beaten, and I also knew there was a good possibility I'd get grounded for something so small as pissing around under the house at night, because Mom is like that—quick with her grounding trigger finger—so I had to think fast. "Hi!" I shouted, trying to sound happy and innocent.

"Who were those boys? I'm carrying a gun! I called the police! They'll be here any second," she screamed. "I could've shot you!"

"Whoops!" I called out.

Then Mom went completely ballistic. I mean she freaked! I think she woke up dogs in like a three-mile radius, because she was freaking so hard. Barking and howling ensued all over the neighborhood. This actually worked to my advantage, because while she was freaking, I realized I could tell her the truth, or at least part of the truth, and that would make her feel dumb and bad for losing her mind like that and carrying around a damn gun!

When we got into the house I said, "Jeez, mom, we were just working on our science project. We were just looking for mold on paper . . ."

"What? You were? With those boys?" Mom asked. Her eyes were bloodshot and her face was bright red.

Lindsey had come out into the living room because she'd heard the screaming (thankfully Dez sleeps like the dead or we'd all be in trouble). "He's telling the truth. I met those guys. They're pretty gross, definitely legitimate eighth graders," she said.

"Yeah. Why did you just go crazy?" I asked.

Mom flopped down on the couch (the gun was still in her hand!). "Oh God, I don't know," she sighed. "I just don't know what to do." Then she sort of started crying, which was normal for her for quite a while after Dad disappeared. Lindsey hugged her. I told them both I was going to bed.

Once I got in bed, I couldn't sleep. First, I felt really shitty for making my mom cry. Second, I was filled with adrenaline. I thought about that gun. No, I wasn't jacked because my own mom might've shot me. I was jacked because of the place where that gun was stored. Mom's antique bureau. It locks. If anybody—specifically Mom or Dad—had anything hugely important to store in the house, they would very likely put it in Mom's closet (totally off limits to kids—she stores candy in there, which she keeps for herself!) and inside of Mom's bureau.

I sat straight up in bed. "I bet Wiz has tools to pick locks in his backpack," I said out loud.

And then, even though it was buried in my closet, even though it sounded miles away, I heard the walkie-talkie say, "I bet he does. I bet he does. I bet he does."

I buried my head in my pillows.

CHAPTER FOURTEEN

Friday. The guest book. The bike. The ghost boy. The hippie . . .

Man, all that shit just dogged me on my winding way to school (I was pretty tired and swerved into traffic and some assholes honked at me). I parked my bike at the rack. I locked it. I thought . . .

The guest book. The bike. The ghost boy. The hippie . . .

And, the walkie-talkie.

Before leaving for school I'd dug it from the closet and I'd put it in my own pack. It hadn't said a word, but it was on me, with me.

Inside school, just before the bell rang, I saw Wiz. He was heading off to the gifted nerd side of the building. He whispered, "Have some information about defending ourselves from that little demon boy."

"You believe, huh?" I said.

He nodded. "We need to find the girl, so we can save her," he whispered. "See you in Earth Science." Wiz had read enough fantasy to see himself as some hero finding and saving a girl, I think. I didn't like it.

Find the girl? She seemed like the least of our problems. I had to find the guest book, because it was Friday, and like Cortez said, Saturday was coming! Saturday meant something! Saturday it would all end! What the fuck would all end? Holy shit!

I was a little jacked, pals.

All morning I stayed to myself. Stayed silent. Didn't look at teachers or classmates. Just kept my head down. Just worried like crazy (I actually looked the same as I did every other day).

Right after lunch, I ran into Mattheson and Mouse outside the Earth Science classroom (where we were all heading).

"Charlie! You should have seen it, bro!" Mattheson cried.

"What?"

"Riley totally got hauled into the principal's office, dude," Mouse said.

"He was smacking his head on a locker really hard. Like, brain crushing hard, okay?" Mattheson said. "And he was laughing!"

"Seriously?" I said. "That's weird. He was so weird yesterday, too."

"Completely weird," Mouse said.

The bell rang. I followed the dudes into the classroom and right away I knew something had been burned in there. Smelled seriously bad. Wiz had gotten to the classroom before us. He stood by Ms. Farhaven's desk, a look of shock on his face. Ms. Farhaven frowned as we entered, which froze Mouse in mid-stride, which caused Mattheson to run into his back.

"What are you doing, bro?" Mattheson said.

"What's wrong, Ms. Farhaven?" Mouse asked.

Ms. Farhaven just said, "Trouble."

Riley bounded into the room and smacked into Mattheson. "Sorry!" he cried. "Had to speak with the principal! He's nice!"

I turned and stared at him. This was a dude who two days ago would barely look up from the floor, would barely mutter a word. Now he sounded like one of the drama kids.

"Follow me, boys," Ms. Farhaven said, somberly. She led us to the supply closet in the back of the room. The other students in the class stared and whispered as we walked past. The room itself reeked of smoke. Ms. Farhaven showed us the source, a plastic bin filled with a moist, mushy black substance. I had to stand on my tiptoes and lean over Mouse and Wiz to see what it was exactly. I couldn't tell.

"What's that?" I asked.

"What's left of your volcano," Ms. Farhaven said. "A janitor had to chase out a vandal last night and he found your project burning."

Mouse looked at Riley then blurted out, "It wasn't Riley!"

"It wasn't?" Riley said.

"I don't think it was Riley," Ms. Farhaven said. "Riley's quiet and thoughtful."

"I am?" Riley asked

Ms. Farhaven turned and looked deep into Mattheson's eyes, then she turned to Mouse. "There's no way you two set some kind of time bomb inside the volcano, right? Because that sort of explosive wouldn't be allowed in school."

"The ass-cano was just plaster, nothing else, Ms. Farhaven," Mouse said. "I swear to you."

"No bombs, Ms. Farhaven," Mattheson said. "Ask Wiz. He examined it."

"No bombs," Wiz said.

Ms. Farhaven stared at Wiz for a moment then shook her head. "Well, I'm so sorry, boys," she said. "Your volcano is gone. I hope you wrote down the plans so you can rebuild it before the presentation."

"No rebuilding!" Riley cried. "The ass is gone!"

We all stared at Riley. Then Wiz spoke. "It's okay. Our project is evolving."

"Good," Ms. Farhaven said. She turned and exited the closet.

"That ass-cano!" Riley said. "I hate ass-canos! Had to burn."

"Riley?" Wiz said.

"Yes, Wizard?" Riley said.

"Are you even in there?" Wiz asked.

Riley just smiled bigger. Then he nudged his head into Wiz's chest.

"Hey, Jesus! Don't do that," Wiz said, pushing Riley back.

"Awww," Riley said. He pouted like my sister pouts when she's faking having her feelings hurt. "Come on, widdle Wizzy."

"Riley, shut up," I said. I turned to the others. "Rooster the ghost boy must've burned our butt."

"No," Riley said.

We all looked at him. He lifted his eyebrows up and down and clicked his tongue. He smiled like a Halloween pumpkin head.

"Did you burn the butt, Riley?" I asked.

"Riley?" Riley said. "Oh no, he would never!"

"Seriously. Are you even Riley?" Wiz said.

"Get the book, Charlie," Riley said. "Get the guest book or else."

"The guest book?" Mouse asked. "Is he talking about what we were looking for last night?"

"Guest book!" Riley shouted.

"Or else what?" I asked.

"The fat man won't help us and one of us will have our souls shredded!" Riley stared straight at me. That giant stupid grin erupted on his face. Then he dipped his head and leaned in close. "Me or you," he whispered. "Me or you."

"Holy fuck," I whispered. "Oh shit."

"We can't talk about this here. Let's meet right after school," Wiz said. "Bike rack."

CHAPTER FIFTEEN

After school, the already way whacked-out Riley met the rest of us by the bike racks. I unlocked my SE right away because I wanted to get off school property before we had what was sure to be a bizarre conversation. I had already put two and two together. Wiz had, too. Even Mouse seemed to be figuring it out.

While I unlocked my bike, Riley smiled, said, "Me or you, Charlie," then he sat down in the yard.

Out of no place the walkie-talkie in my pack came alive. "Who said that?" it asked.

Mouse stared at me. I shrugged. "Walkie-talkie," I said.

Then Mouse turned to Riley. "Bro. You're scaring the shit out of everybody."

I rolled my bike over to Riley. "Me worst of all," I said.

Riley nodded and smiled. "Very scary."

I knew it. Wiz knew it. Mouse sort of knew it. Someone or something had taken over Riley's controls. "Who said that?" asked the walkie-talkie in my pack. I decided not to answer. I stared at Riley.

Truth is, Riley didn't even control his own face. He wasn't the one who nodded at all. He wasn't the one who robbed Little Debbies from a convenience store the day before. Riley was some place in there, but he wasn't driving his own body!

This is pretty hard to report and be confident I'm telling the truth. But here it is, the shit Riley told us all later about what happened.

During the night after we met at the Oceannaire, the ghost girl had slid into him. It wasn't a dream like before. It was real. He'd woken at 3 a.m., wind blowing through Hoover and Memaw's living room, blowing over a lamp, scattering newspaper all over. He couldn't move. Couldn't scream. The girl entered in through the window. Slowly approached him, fully formed, glowing white, floating. "You said you'd help," she whispered. "It's time." She lay flat against him. He nearly froze from the cold. "Thank you," she said. She shut her eyes, rolled tight, then shot up his damn nose! He sat up fast, released from whatever power locked him in place before. He cried out. Slapped his face. Breathed. The wind had stopped. He wasn't cold. He thought, *must be another nightmare,* although it had seemed so real. He lay down and fell back asleep.

When the sun woke our boy up, he definitely felt displaced and a little weird, like he'd been through something big. Nothing too out of the ordinary, though, because Riley often had bad dreams and ever since he moved to Encinitas, away from his family home back in Utah, he'd felt sort of displaced.

But the weird feeling got weirder.

Wiz, Mouse and Mattheson hadn't seen Riley at school Thursday (their only class with him was Ms. Farhaven's in the afternoon), but Riley had, in fact, gone to school. Sitting in his early classes Riley had slowly gotten the impression that he was looking at reality through a pair of binoculars. Everything—blackboard, classmates, Shakespeare posters—in his Language Arts class with Mr. Zimmerman looked close, but felt super far away. Mr. Zimmerman actually stopped his lecture on metaphors at one point and asked him why he was blinking so much. "I'm blinking?" Riley had replied, because he didn't know.

By the time he got to gym, right before lunch, he was feeling completely detached from the tactile world. Weird things were going down. He could reach out and touch a metal school door, but he didn't *feel* the metal. When he peed, he didn't get the sensation of peeing—he actually got the sensation that someone was peeing for him (and enjoying it). Then in gym, during a game of dodge ball, which he normally hated, Landon Anderson had blasted him in the face. Instead of falling to the ground and balling up into a fetal zero like our boy would normally do, he screamed, reached down, grabbed a ball, reared back, and absolutely obliterated Landon, like threw the ball so hard it bounced off Landon's head and shot up to the ceiling.

Landon fell over on his face. He lay there. Mr. Carlson, the gym teacher, paused for a moment, because he'd never seen anybody throw a damn ball that hard. He was all like, "That was beautiful!" But then he recovered himself enough to realize Riley had broken the rules, stayed in the game after being knocked out, stayed in the game just to retaliate, and Carlson began to shout at Riley to get off the damn court unless he wanted to stay after class.

Riley stared at pissed-off Mr. Carlson. Riley's mouth snarled. Riley's body trembled with rage. Riley's mouth shouted, "Stick it, baldy!" Then he took off at a dead sprint and ran into a wall and fell backwards. Everybody laughed. He got up and ran right out of the building.

Weird as shit, because Riley wasn't positive he was running, even though his body felt like it was running.

He got to his dumbass beach cruiser. He got on the bike. He rode his bike, but the whole time had the sensation that he wasn't the one riding at all.

Holy shit, he thought. *AM I HAVING A STROKE? AM I DYING?* This thought repeated again and again. *HOLY SHIT! HOLY SHIT! HOLY SHIT!*

The bike picked up speed, flew down a hill, went faster than cars, careened in and out of traffic. Riley could do nothing to stop himself, dudes.

HOLY SHIT! OH SHIT JESUS OH MY GOD! he cried in his head.

Then the bike, seemingly of its own accord, pulled to the side of a busy street. Riley's body breathed deep. A girl's voice said, "Just relax. You're fine." But, Riley couldn't see this girl.

Who said that? he thought. *What the hell?*

"Shh," the girl's voice said.

ARE YOU IN MY HEAD? he thought. *DOESN'T THAT MEAN I'M DEFINITELY HAVING A STROKE? HELP!* he cried silently.

"Let's do some stuff, okay?" the girl's voice said. "Some super stuff."

NO! WHAT'S GOING ON? HELP!!!

"Shhhhh . . ."

And there was no saying no. Suddenly our boy was along for a ride on an adventure he did not want to be on. During the afternoon, his body jumped higher than it possibly could (from the curb to up on top of a strip mall for instance). His body broke stuff in stores, stole stuff in stores, scared old ladies on the street, all while this girl's voice shrieked in delight. He vaguely remembered showing up at a park and shouting at Wiz, Mouse, Mattheson and me. He also remembered his body flipping us the bird. Right after that, Riley got so upset—inside his body, he'd tried to shout to us, to beg us for help—he believes he lost consciousness. He doesn't know what his body did the rest of the day (bad stuff for sure —he got in the school and burned shit), while his soul stayed fast asleep . . .

This is the next thing he knows for sure: he woke up in the morning lying on the couch in Hoover and Memaw's living room. Again, he figured he'd just had an epically bad dream. He wasn't exactly sure what day it was. Then his body got up without him doing any work. His body peed and a girl's voice said, "Standing and peeing is the best!" He biked to school without feeling the sensations of biking. *SHE* was in control.

It was at school that the girl inside him started getting super upset. He could hear her mumbling. "Charlie Wilkins better find that book or we're done. Riley Riley Riley we better get that book that guest book or the earth will get shaky and they'll cut you like a chicken and turn me to shreds."

What? Riley asked. *What book? A guest book?*

"We need the guest book!" Riley's mouth screamed.

Kids in the hall stared at him in total horror.

"Only the fat man can teach us what to do!" Riley's mouth shrieked.

WHAT? WHAT? Riley screamed in his thoughts.

Then the girl began to smack his head into a locker over and over until a teacher came, grabbed his hand, walked him to the principal's office, where, oddly, the girl was on her best behavior. She called Principal Griffith "sir," and apologized for creating a ruckus—said she was trying to make a dumb joke—and asked to go back to class. Principal Griffith accepted this apology. (He wouldn't have if he had seen the security camera videotape—again, there was one old-school VHS camera that had functioned properly that had captured "Riley" breaking into the school during the night and setting a fire in Ms. Farhaven's room.) Riley, and the girl who animated him, made it out of the principal's office just in time to get to Earth Science, to meet up with us, to say those scary-ass things.

Scary-ass things that continued to fall out of his mouth when we met outside after school.

Riley sat on the lawn. We all surrounded him. Again he said, "Me or you, Charlie Wilkins."

"Yeah. I get it," I said.

"Unless we find the guest book," Riley said.

Wiz kneeled down next to him. He spoke softly. "What do you know?" Wiz asked.

"Everything?" Riley's mouth said. "Except some stuff. That stuff is in the guest book at Charlie's house."

"How do you know about that book, Riley?" I asked.

Riley's face flushed. He swallowed. "I'm very hungry," Riley said. "I want a cheeseburger."

"Are we in danger?" I asked. "For real? Do you know that?"

Riley nodded. "Me or you, Charlie Wilkins of the sixth generation. Me or you." Riley stood fast then fell over backwards.

"Whoa!" Mouse said.

"Cheeseburger now!" Riley said, sitting back up. "The energy is low. Very low."

Wiz moved close to Riley again, spoke quietly again. "Are we speaking to Riley or to someone else?" he asked.

Riley smiled, "I am someone."

Wiz pointed at Mouse and Mattheson. He said, "Did you happen to meet these guys before? Tuesday night, maybe?"

Riley's eyes stared at the dudes. His head slowly nodded. "Oh dang," he said. "It was supposed to be Wednesday, but I sucked the batteries too soon. Those boys . . ." he pointed at Mouse and Mattheson ". . . felt like Riley, but they weren't Riley when I found them."

Wiz turned to me. He nodded. I nodded back. We were thinking the same thing. He turned back to Riley's body. "Is your name Paula, by any chance?"

Riley's head lit up like a beach fire. I mean, what a freaking crazy grinning pumpkin head, okay? "Yes!" he shouted. "You know me! I'm me! I'm here! I'm Paula!"

"Oh whoa," Mouse muttered. "Balls, dude."

"She's the ghost girl? She's in Riley?" Mattheson said. "That is so sick."

"Paula? You're Paula?" I thought of Rooster, what he said. "You're Paula of the fifth generation? The one Rooster was talking about," I whispered.

Suddenly the light drained from Riley (Paula). He trembled, sank to the ground. "Do you have people food? A cheeseburger?" Paula inside Riley whispered. "The energy is going low."

Wiz reached into his bag and pulled out an energy bar. Then he said to me, Mouse, and Mattheson, "I'm going to give Riley . . . I mean Paula this. That should get him off the ground. Then we better make plans."

"Cheeseburger," Riley's mouth whispered. "I have a tongue."

"Soon," Wiz said. Then Wiz opened the energy bar, broke off a chunk and stuck it in Riley's mouth. Riley's mouth chewed and chewed.

"More?" Riley's mouth said.

Wiz pulled out the rest of the bar and put it in Riley's hand. Riley's hand jammed the whole thing into Riley's mouth. The mouth chewed more. "Pretty good," he (she) said, mouth completely full.

"Let's go to my gramps' workshop. I need to build a ghost zapper," Wiz said. "We can figure out what's next from there."

Suddenly, there was the sound of static coming from my backpack. A voice, probably the hippie's, said, "Got the guest book? Over. Guest book, Charlie?" There was more static. I just didn't want to talk to Cortez. I really didn't like the hippie, you know? I made no move to get the walkie-talkie out.

"Jesus! Dude! What is that noisy shit that keeps coming from your pack?" Mouse said.

Riley's body sat up off the ground fast. "Guest book!" Riley cried.

I looked over at Wiz. "Do you happen to have any lock picking tools or maybe skeleton keys in your bag, dude?"

"Uh, yeah?" he said.

I had to look in Mom's drawer for the guest book before I did anything else. No, I didn't like Cortez and I didn't want to do what he wanted me to do. Riley stared at me, eyes wide. Paula knew about the guest book, too. I just knew I had to find that damn book.

CHAPTER SIXTEEN

We decided to split up. Mouse and Mattheson went with Wiz back to his place. Apparently Wiz's gramps had given him some instructions for reverse engineering a cow prod into a ghost zapper. Seemed as reasonable as anything. We might really have to do battle with ghosts before the coming dawn, right? That was like fourteen hours away! I decided to take Riley with me, because I figured Paula might be able to sense if we were getting close to the guest book. She was definitely attuned to the notion we needed to find it, right? Before we left the school, Riley (Paula) begged Mouse to use his skateboard. "I was the best skater in my neighborhood," she (he) said.

"Uh, I would not like to say yes, but I'm scared of you," Mouse said.

"Okay!" Riley's face said.

Then Riley skated like he was disco dancing on a 1970s TV show. He was smooth as shit, to be honest.

And, even though we went up hill for a good part of the way and I was on a bike, Riley/Paula had little trouble keeping up with me on the skateboard. It was like Paula's ghost energy super-powered him. Or was he even him at all? I thought that as we rolled. Was Riley actually okay? I wondered if he was still inside of himself or if he'd been knocked out to hell or something? Going up a big hill, I asked:

"Hey, Paula? Where is the actual kid named Riley, you know? The owner of the body?"

"He's here," Paula said.

"Okay, good," I said. That was a relief.

"I don't want him to go away. He's my friend. So he's here to stay!" Paula said.

"Is he okay?" I asked. "Like comfortable?"

Paula paused for a second. She kicked on the board so she was in front of me. I caught up.

"Seriously. Is he okay?" I asked.

"I don't know. I'll ask," Paula said. "Hey, are you okay in there?" she said. She nodded like she was listening to somebody then said, "He's pretty mad because I keep making him do crazy stuff and if I harm his body he's going to be really, really mad at me, but yeah he's okay sort of otherwise."

"Ha! All right. Good," I said. Not like I could do anything if Riley was in pain. It was a relief to know he wasn't on fire or something.

We got to my house a few minutes later.

After I pulled in the garage, Paula said, "I think I lived near here. Where are we? What day is it?" She dropped the board next to my bike. "Is today Friday?"

"I lived in a house. I'm a girl."

"I guess. True," I said. I had to agree, but it was weird to be staring at big Riley while Paula said that.

Then she scrunched his eyes and looked up, like she was thinking really hard. "You know, I feel like I'm me, but then I'm not me, because I'm not just Paula the girl."

I shook my head. "No," I said.

She looked down and stared me in the face. "Charlie Wilkins, there's a ghost in the girl."

"There's a ghost in Riley."

"There's a ghost in me. It's me. Don't be scared. There's a ghost in the girl." She nodded. She swallowed hard.

I don't know how to explain it, but that was about the saddest thing I'd ever heard anybody say. Thankfully she had a hard time staying on track.

She looked past me. "Hey. Is this your house?" she asked.

I exhaled, nodded and motioned for her to follow me.

I nodded and motioned for her to follow me.

We entered through the garage door and went straight into the kitchen.

"It smells good in here. Like a family. Like a mom and kids. It doesn't smell like a man. Is there no man? Wait, you're Charlie Wilkins, right?" Paula asked.

"Yeah, you know that. You've been calling me Charlie Wilkins all day," I said.

"I have? We've been together? What day is it?" Riley's voice got louder and louder.

"Keep it down, okay? I don't want to draw attention to ourselves."

"But if you're Charlie Wilkins then your dad is gone. He's not here, so that's why I can't smell a man in this . . ."

"Shut up," I said. "Don't say another damn word. I don't know what you're . . . what you're even talking about."

"Because Rooster wouldn't come after you if your dad was in this world."

It was like getting slapped. "Shut up!" I shouted.

So much for not drawing attention to us. Lindsey heard me from the living room where she was watching TV. "What's your problem, Charlie?" she yelled.

I put my finger in front of my mouth then pointed at Paula. I glared. "I don't know what you're talking about, but you have to keep your voice down, or else. Do you understand?" I whispered.

"Yeah!" Paula said, pretty damn loudly. Then she pumpkin smiled, which made me want to kill her, because I was already trembling, because how did she know my dad was gone? And what did she mean he wasn't in this world?

I had to get it together. I exhaled. I said, "Follow me."

We got past the living room and Dez and Lindsey without any problem. They were both glued to the TV. The real trouble (if the guest book was even in the bureau in Mom's closet) was Mom, herself. She would leave for work in an hour. Given that fact, it was pretty likely she was in her room or the attached bathroom getting dressed or showering, which would mean we'd have to wait, which would mean I'd have to keep ghost girl/bizarre boy from doing anything wicked crazy in the house for longer. I didn't want that.

Even though Mom didn't seem to be anywhere else, I knocked on her bedroom door. Riley's body was right behind me. He leaned his nose into my neck and said, "You smell good."

"Shh," I said.

Mom didn't answer her door, so I turned the knob and poked my head into the room. The radio (hits of the 80s and 90s!) played some evil sounding song about having a white wedding. I stretched out my neck and scanned. Mom wasn't there. I took a step in. Riley followed. The shower went on in the bathroom attached to her room. "We can do this," I whispered.

"Super!" Riley/Paula said.

"We have to move fast, though."

If I had a different mom, a more leisurely one, the timing might have been perfect. But Mom takes short showers. She thinks that people who take a long time in there are lazy or something. If I take a long shower, she always says, "I thought you went down the drain." (That's scary when you're a little kid, by the way.) I was serious when I said we had to move fast.

I shot across the room, threw open the closet door, leapt deep into the back. Riley's body followed. I told him to shut the door. He did. "Smells like a lady," Paula said into the darkness.

"Don't talk about my mom," I said.

Then I pulled out my phone and tried to use the flashlight, but the thing wouldn't turn on (smart phones don't function around full-blown ghosts like Paula). Luckily, I knew that mom kept a flashlight in the closet. I'd seen it before when going in there to steal candies. I reached up, grabbed two little Snickers and the flashlight (right next to the candy bag, right where I knew it would be). I turned it on and handed one Snicker to Riley.

"Oh God, yes!" Paula shouted.

"You quiet down now, dude," I hissed. I shined the light right in his/her face.

The pumpkin face nodded. "Sorry."

"Dig around a little. See if you find the book, okay? I'm going to try to get into this old bureau."

I stuck the back end of the flashlight in my mouth and illuminated the floor in front of me. I pulled the little box of Wiz's skeleton keys out of my pocket then knelt down in front of the antique bureau where mom kept dad's gun and her jewelry box and where I figured she might keep some weird, powerful book dad had asked her to squirrel away. I pulled open the box. There were a bunch of little screwdrivers and bobby pins clipped on one side. There were ten different skeleton keys piled on the other side. Wiz seemed to think that one of the skeleton keys would work.

While Riley ate more Snickers (he immediately found the bag), I pulled out a key. Shined the light on it. Shined the light on the drawer. I tried the key. It slid into the lock really easily and for a tenth of a second I thought maybe

I'd hit the damn jackpot. Unfortunately, though, the key wouldn't turn. "Shit," I whispered. "Shit," said a voice above me.

"Ahh!" Riley/Paula shouted.

"Ahh!" shouted the voice.

I leapt up. I shined my light around the closet. "Is there someone else in here?" I whispered.

"Is there someone else in here?" the voice said.

I raised the beam of the flashlight to the shelves. It landed on a stuffed, battery-powered parrot.

Remember when Cortez said that Dad had set up a cloak, something to do with a bird? In retrospect, I think this was it, this damn parrot. It had been a birthday gift for Lindsey a few years ago. The thing repeated what you said. But dad, or somebody, had done something to it. The parrot's eyes began to glow red.

"Jesus," I whispered.

"Jesus," the parrot said.

"Is that alive?" Paula asked.

"Is that alive?" The parrot said. "Scanning. Scanning. Scanning."

"Scanning?" I asked.

"Scanning complete," the parrot said. "Wilkins. You are Wilkins and you are Kelly. Be careful. Be careful. Yankee Jim! Yankee Jim! Do not take the book. You be careful. Squawk!"

"Yankee Jim?" There was that damn name again! It made my stomach twist. I reached up, grabbed the parrot (it screeched), turned it over and pulled out the batteries. "Shut up, bird."

"That bird said my name," Paula said.

"No it didn't," I said.

I put the parrot back on the shelf then bent down and fiddled with the lock again. The second key fit in the lock, too, but didn't work. The third was too big to go in the hole. The fourth was clearly too small, but I tried anyway. The fifth was, again, too big.

"It did say my name," Paula said, chewing another Snickers.

"Be quiet," I said.

I began to sweat, pals. *Bird says Yankee Jim. Mom is almost done showering.* I was running out of key options fast. But then the sixth key. I pulled it out of the box, shined the light on it, eyeballed the tip. It looked like the same shape as the drawer lock. I mean, I could see it! I stuck the key in, heard a click, the key sliding into some mechanism within. I turned the key and it worked. "Holy shit," I whispered.

"Holy shit?" said Riley.

I pulled open the drawer, cool air poured out. And there, in the darkness at the bottom of the drawer, sat a leather bound book. "Riley. I mean Paula. Is this the book?" I shined the flashlight on the thing.

"Yes, Charlie!" Paula said. "That's it!"

"Yankee Jim, Charlie Wilkins! Do not take the book!" said the parrot, which made me jump and hit my head on a shelf, because goddamn it, I turned that bird off less than a minute before. I pulled out its batteries! What the hell?

The door to the bathroom squeaked in mom's bedroom. She was out! I shined the flashlight on my face and gestured to Riley to be quiet. The music we'd been able to hear coming from mom's radio stopped playing. She'd turned it off.

I held my breath. I could hear my heart beating in my chest. *Shut up, heart!* I thought.

Okay, you know what? My run-in with the ghost boy Rooster had scared me quite a damn bit, but not nearly as much as my mom could scare me when she totally freaked, which she definitely would if she found me and some random fat boy in her closet, especially after finding me under the house the night before.

I closed the book drawer with my foot and backed myself into the corner next to the bureau. I shined the flashlight on Riley/Paula's face and gestured that he should back up to the corner on the other side. Freaking miracle, the dude (or girl) understood me. Riley stepped across the closet and backed into the corner. We both pulled hanging clothes up against us. I even reached down and pulled a pair of my mom's big undies onto my shoes. Right then the door began to swing open. I shut off the flashlight quick. *Please don't hear my heart!* I thought.

Mom, singing "Girls Just Wanna Have Fun" to herself, stepped in.

The parrot said, "Want to have fun!"

"How did you turn on, you stupid parrot?" Mom said.

"Stupid parrot! Stupid parrot!" the parrot said. "Wilkins!"

"Ha! Good memory!" she said.

"Wilkins! Book!" the parrot cried.

Mom groaned, "World's most annoying toy."

I made myself as thin as possible, shut my eyes tight. I tried not to let the terror of the battery-less parrot affect me. *Shh . . . Shh . . .* I thought.

Mom grabbed something off a high shelf (*probably scrubs*, I figured) and then was gone. She shut the door behind her.

I breathed, but the danger was far from done. First, Mom was out there in the bedroom. Second, Riley/ Paula could do something weird. He/she did. Paula (or whoever) whispered, "Your mom is naked." And, third, the parrot, because the parrot screeched, "Naked!" I pushed my head out between hanging clothes, snapped on the flashlight, aimed it at my face and again gestured to be quiet. Then snapped the flashlight back off.

"Why?" Riley/Paula asked.

"Why?" The possessed parrot chimed in.

"Shh . . ." I said.

And yeah, I was right to shush, because the door flew open and mom stomped in. At least she had scrubs on. She grabbed the parrot off the top shelf and hissed, "I've had enough of you."

"Enough of them," the parrot said. "Enough of the Wilkins boy."

"You!" she shouted. She sort of strangled it, smashed it on the door frame. Then she turned and stomped out.

Oh man, did I want to get that guest book and get the hell out of there.

Mom does stuff fast. She was clothed. It was almost go time. I counted to twenty-five. I counted to fifty. She was definitely out of her bedroom by a hundred.

Just go.

I knelt down again, flipped on my flashlight, pulled open the massive drawer and picked up the guest book. The thing weighed a ton. "Okay. Okay. Oh shit," I whispered. "This is it, right?" I asked Riley. "This is definitely the book?"

Nobody answered.

I stood and poked around in the hanging clothes. Riley wasn't in the closet. Or else he was hiding really damn well. "Hey. You here?" I asked.

"Kelly is gone. Kelly is gone," the smashed battery-less parrot said from Mom's bedroom.

And then I heard a knocking sound, like maybe someone was knocking on the window out there. I scrambled to the front of the closet, pushed open the door and looked out. And holy balls, baby Jesus! Riley's smiling, bobbing, pumpkin head stared back at me from outside the damn house!

I slid out of the closet. I climbed on my parents' bed, kicked the battery-less parrot (that had its electronics all pulled apart—Mom's work) to the ground, and opened the bedroom window.

"What the hell are you doing?" I whispered.

"Hi!" Paula said. "How are you?"

"How did you get outside?" I asked.

Paula shrugged. She Riley-style pumpkin smiled. "Why don't you give me that book?" she said. "I'll carry it away and it will be safe."

"Careful! Careful! Yankee Jim!" cried the parrot from the floor.

"If you go through the house, your mom might see you with it," Riley said.

"Do not take the book!" cried the parrot.

I handed the book through the window.

Riley grabbed it. "I'll go!" Riley said. "Bye bye!"

"Careful Kelly! Careful!" cried the parrot.

"Meet me outside!" I shouted, but Riley was already bounding away like some kind of antelope/orangutan monster man. "Stop!" I cried.

Riley didn't stop. He shot across the yard and into the neighbors'. He ran around a corner, behind some tall bushes.

"Crap!" I said.

"The book is gone," said the parrot.

I rolled off the bed and tore out of the bedroom into the hall.

Mom sat next to Dez on the couch in the living room. I slowed down, kissed her cheek, said, "Going to hang out with friends, okay?"

"Good!" she said. "Good!" She'd been pretty worried about my lack of human contact over the course of the preceding months, so that was lucky.

I had to catch Riley. Who knows where the crazed dude might go? I ran to the garage, grabbed my SE, jumped on it and pedaled out into the street. Suddenly my phone began buzzing (it hadn't picked up any texts while I was in close proximity to haunted Riley and the parrot. They all came at once).

We're in back of my house, workshop. Follow path behind house, Wiz wrote.

Oh yeah, address: 1143 La Noria, he wrote.

Get here fast. I just thought of something, Wiz wrote.

Right then my phone went dead again.

"Hi Charlie!" Riley/Paula said. "Look at this! I found the book!" He held up the guest book like it was something I probably never saw before.

"You found it, huh?" I said. "Good for you."

"Wait," Riley's face said. "What day is it? Is it Friday?"

I nodded slowly.

"Oh dang, Charlie Wilkins. Saturday is the day after Friday. Don't forget. Don't forget that. Charlie Wilkins you don't forget that it's Friday!" Riley's eyes went wide. "Don't forget Saturday morning!"

"I won't forget. We're getting ready to fight. Come with me, Paula," I said.

"We have to fight for all the generations. You go fast as you can, Charlie Wilkins," Riley's face said. "I can skateboard super fast!"

"All the generations? What are you talking about?" I asked.

Riley had already pulled the skateboard out of the garage and launched into his Paula sexy disco skating. He was off!

He was going in the wrong direction.

CHAPTER SEVENTEEN

"So, ghosts pretty much suck energy out of stuff. They love ion batteries. That's why our cell phones stop working around Riley. That's what Gramps told me, anyway," Wiz said to Mouse and Mattheson.

"Oh! I've got a little charge now, but my phone was pretty much full before we saw Riley. I charged it in reading class," Mouse said.

"Yeah," Wiz said.

"I don't get it," Mattheson said.

"You don't have to, bro," Mouse said.

They stood around Gramps' giant worktable waiting for me and Riley to arrive with the guest book. Wiz wore his goggles. Gramps' Magrath Stock Shock sat on the table to his right. In front of him sat an 80-watt bug zapper. He had a back panel opened and was messing with the electronics inside. His goal was to reverse the energy flow in the thing. "Bug zappers fry. Ghosts might actually benefit from that jolt of energy. Not like it could harm their bodies, because they're disembodied."

"Oh?" Mattheson said.

"We should be able to get the energy to flow in the other direction though. Gramps has already made this cattle prod thing that will suck a ghost's energy into zero, making them incapable of movement or action. With this car battery hooked up to this bug zapper, and a similar reverse course, I bet we can discharge a bunch of ghosts all at once."

"Do you have any food?" Mattheson asked.

Riley (Paula) and I parked my bike next to an old, rusted out Ford pickup truck (the other cars in the driveway were a Lexus SUV and the BMW we'd seen Wiz get out of at the Oceannaire. I personally liked the pickup best). We followed Wiz's instructions, walked up a path behind the giant glass house.

"Skinny man watching," Riley's head said.

"A ghost? What?" I asked, freezing.

"No. A real man," Riley turned and pointed. I followed the line of Riley's hand. Sure enough, a tall, middle-aged dude, illuminated by one of the house's floodlights, stood on a balcony outside of Wiz's house. I waved at him. He seemed to raise the glass in his hand, a little bit, anyway, at least acknowledged he saw us.

"Must be Wiz's dad," I said.

We turned and hoofed it back up the path. I could see lights ahead of us, maybe a hundred yards or so. Looked like we were walking into a campground at night. Super dark. The shadows from trees shifted a bit because of a breeze.

"I like my body," Paula said.

"Uh, it's not your body," I said.

"I know."

We got to the workshop, which looked more like a little, fancy two-story house. I think Wiz had called it a shack. You'd have to be a damn rich boy to think that place was a shack. It was more like something from a fairytale or from Disneyland (a home for the seven dwarves). I looked through the window into the workshop part of the house in time to see Mouse and Mattheson cover their eyes while Wiz zapped the bug zapper with an arc welder. I looked away. Riley/Paula stared right at it. "Pretty!" he said.

"Don't look at it. You'll burn out Riley's eyes."

"Whoops!" Paula said

After Wiz was done with the next small weld, I entered a door to our right and walked into the shop. "What's happening?"

"Did you find the book?" Mattheson asked, uncovering his eyes.

Riley entered behind me. His hand held up the giant book. "Here!" Paula shouted.

"Keep it down. Gramps is watching a movie upstairs," Wiz said.

"Okay!" Paula shouted again.

Wiz stared at Riley's face. "Okay. We've made some advancements. I think I have a way to suck the energy out of a ghost from a distance of ten feet," Wiz said. "If I turn this thing on . . ."

"Don't!" screamed Riley's face.

"Be quiet," I hissed.

"Don't suck my energy! Please!" Paula cried.

"I think you're protected, because you're inside of a biological entity," Wiz said.

"Paula calm down, okay? Can we get a look into the book?" I asked.

Riley's body plopped the book down on the table even while Riley's face stayed stricken. The book settled, sighed as it sat on the table. There was definitely something weird about it, something almost alive (I stared at it, and I swear I could see it breathe).

Riley began to jump up and down. "Oh. Ooh. That thing's hot. Okay!" Paula said from his face. Again, she was very loud. Gramps couldn't be enjoying the movie with Riley's ruckus.

"Hey, Mouse, Mattheson, why don't you take Riley outside? Turn on the back light. Gramps has a beanbag toss game out there," Wiz said without once looking up from the book.

"A what the hell, bro?" Mattheson asked.

"Beanbag. You throw little sacks of beans through a hole in a target," Wiz said.

"What, dude?" Mouse said.

Riley jumped so high his head smacked into the ceiling.

"Okay. Let's go outside," Mattheson said, staring at Riley.

As soon as they were out the door, Wiz pushed the ghost zapper machine to his left and re-lowered his cracked goggles. He pulled on a pair of work gloves "just in case" and opened the book. I swear I heard a sigh. I swear I saw a little plume of smoke rise up. The book seemed to expand.

Wiz hunched over the first pages. He pulled out a stack of old newspaper clippings and other notes and slid it across the table towards me. "Look at that stuff," he said. So I sat across from him, studying the stack of yellowed newsprint.

There was also tracing paper, sort of thin, see-through, waxy paper I remember playing with when I was a kid (I'd make outlines of Dad's star maps). All that weird old paper had lines drawn all over it.

I studied.

Wiz studied.

I think both our sets of eyes got bigger and bigger.

In fact, later on Wiz told me he couldn't believe what he was seeing. Yes, at first glance, the book seemed to contain regular Whaley House guest book stuff, same kind of crap you'd find at any little museum or at the embarrassing bed and breakfasts my parents made us stay in when we visited my cousins in Portland back in fifth grade (nothing like sharing a historically accurate brothel madam's bedroom with your parents and your big sister—true story). There were pages filled with little notes from people who had visited.

They said things like:

Great tour! My family loves old stuff!
Knowledgeable guides! Fun!!
Fascinating view into the past!
So spooky! Love the ghost stories!
Wonderful window into the old west life of 19th
    century SoCal!

They were signed by people from around the country:

Bob Beemus, NYC
Richard Wilkins, Encinitas (!!!!!!!!!) (Yeah,
    exclamations, because guess . . .)
Sherri Ross and family, Carson City, Nevada
Ricky Van Dinkles, Mt. Pubis, Ida-HO (Wiz
    figured that was a joke.)
Etc. Etc. Etc.

The names went on for thirty pages, or thereabouts. And so, at first, the book didn't seem very special to Wiz. But then he turned ahead a few pages and found a long, garbled note in really weird handwriting. He read it through. He read it again. He tried to understand it, because something sounded familiar.

The cycle is nearly ended. The time has nearly come.
One good shake and the money is gone. The tunnels
below are cracked and crumbling and so soon we

will be watching the underbellies float up into the town, eating the souls and cindering the homes of those strange boys . . .

The scrawling handwriting became completely illegible at that point, but it went on and on.

Scary. It was like some kind of a messed up warning. To whom, though? To visitors of the Whaley House? Those strange boys? Who were the boys? Who would read it? It might be something my dad would read and understand. Maybe something Cortez would understand. When Wiz pointed it out to me later, it definitely didn't occur to me that *we* were the boys, but that might've been the case (Paula told Riley about some prophecy, right?). Anyway, Wiz didn't get it at all.

He turned a few more pages. There were more odd, scribbled notes and sketches that looked like the kind of thing psycho killers would paint on their victims' bedroom walls.

SLICE NICE AND THE BITCH'S BLOOD WILL MAKE WHOLE!

Wiz lost his breath for a moment.

At the same time, I was getting my own balls scared off. I broke the silence. "Man. The papers that were stuck in the book, dude. They're crazy-ass."

"Let me see," Wiz said. I didn't know it, but he actually wanted to look away from the book for a bit, from all the nastiness in there.

I slid a stack of newsprint across the table to him. The pages must've been crushed tight, because, seriously, they continued to expand, like they were greater in number now that they were outside the binding. Wiz began to page through.

"Oh, man," Wiz said.

"Do you remember some of these news stories?" I asked.

"Definitely," Wiz said.

There were newspaper clippings regarding incidents we both recalled growing up: fiery truck crashes off Highway 101, building collapses on the Mexican border, shipwrecks just off the coast, planes that fell from the damn sky, mysterious disappearances of kids from prominent families in the area. And all of these events were stapled on top of these 1980s old-school telex printings that both included what looked like runs of computer code and also short messages like:

```
"demon psych ward unfortunately loosed-
probable cause of death."
```

and

```
"alien craft malfunction set garages
ablaze-unknown, but potent fuel quality
likely cause of accelerated burn."
```

"What in the world is going on here?" Wiz whispered.

"I know," I said. "Dad told me lots of what we can't explain has paranormal origins."

Yeah, pals. But it was more than just "lots." According to these documents (that fell out of this museum guest book), most of the horrible shit that went down in Southern California during our lifetime had paranormal causes.

"No. No," Wiz said, shaking his head, spreading different news stories on Gramps' table in front of him. "This is ridiculous. This isn't real, Charlie. If he's mixed up with this, your dad is crazy, okay? I'm sorry to be the bearer of bad news, but . . ."

By that time, I'd pulled the book over to me and had begun to read signatures. "Shit. Dude. My dad signed the book. So did a Cortez. Harry Cortez. I bet that's the fat hippie. Get this. In his message he wrote, 'Great to visit my family!'"

Wiz looked up. "Visit his family? Do you mean he visited *with* his family?" Wiz asked.

"That's not what Cortez wrote," I said. "'*Great to visit my family.*'"

I tried to think it through. Could Cortez have family working at Whaley House? Could there be some kind of paranormal entity related to Cortez that resided there? Uh, yeah. That maybe made sense.

Meanwhile, Wiz poured through tiny, smudged words on old newsprint. He had to pull up his goggles and blink a bunch because he thought his eyes were going to burn out. He focused again. He saw it. A name, a face, a piece of tracing paper with pencil sketches on it, a telex report that had recently been printed out, some seriously weird numbers scrawled out on the back of the telex next to the name Harry C . . . "Oh my God. Holy shit. I've totally got something," Wiz said. He held up the telex page marked December 9, which was just a day before my dad disappeared. It was stapled to the ancient tracing paper and a newspaper clipping from 1980. The headline in the news clip read: MURDERER TUNNELED INTO TEEN'S BEDROOM. Wiz turned the telex page to the clip so I could see. "Check this out."

I squinted at the yellowed page. "That's over thirty years old. What's the connection to my dad?"

"To your dad?" Wiz asked.

Of course, I hadn't told him about the date or about Dad's disappearance. I tried to cover. "What? Is Cortez mentioned? Did he murder a teen or something?"

The walkie-talkie in my pack popped. I put my finger in front of my mouth. It was possible Cortez was listening to everything we said.

Wiz talked more quietly, but with huge intensity. "No, man. This article is about our science project. This is Riley! I mean the thing inside Riley!" He held the article out, close to my face. "Look at that picture!"

"Yeah. It's the murdered girl," I said. "She's blonde."

"It's her! It's Paula!" Wiz said.

Whoa. I grabbed the newspaper clipping from Wiz's hand. I read the caption. "Holy shit. Her name *is* Paula. Paula Kelly." Suddenly the sound of the parrot from my mom's closet echoed in my ears. "The parrot!" I shouted. "The parrot kept yelling about Kelly!' The parrot said 'Kelly is gone!' The parrot knew her last name!"

Wiz stared at me. "Parrot?"

"The toy parrot my dad must have set up to protect the book!"

Wiz looked down at the table and thought. "Parrot. Paula Kelly. She said you or her. The ghost kid said you or her. But she's already dead. She was murdered. By somebody who came into her house through a tunnel. You're not dead! What the hell's going on?" Wiz said.

"I don't know," I said. "Maybe we should ask Paula damn Kelly? She's at the center of this."

"But she's a ghost. And she's confused. She can't remember what day it is. We do need . . ." Wiz paused. "We need help. Why haven't we contacted Cortez about this book?" Wiz asked. He shook his head. He was getting jumpy as shit. "I mean, we have it. He knows about it. He wants it. It's Friday night. Saturday's coming fast. Paula Kelly, the murdered ghost girl who a little demon boy says we're not supposed to help or save, but who has lodged herself in the body of one of our science project partners so we have to save her, keeps saying we have to do something before Saturday, just like Cortez did."

"Yeah," I said. "Right."

"So, what do we have to do?" Wiz asked. "Why haven't we asked Cortez? We have a walkie-talkie directly linked to the dude. Why haven't we made contact?"

"Because we don't trust his ass?" I said. "My dad didn't. I'm pretty sure."

"Right. We don't trust Cortez," Wiz said. He started talking really fast, whispering, really. "But who can we trust? My gramps, maybe, but there's only so far he's going to go. I doubt he's an expert, too, although he'll act like an expert, and also he'll protect me if he thinks I'm getting in trouble or in danger. He'll tell my parents. He'll make it so I can't help."

That notion sent me into a mini-panic. I needed Wiz! "No. No way. Don't tell him anything."

Wiz swallowed hard. He nodded. "How about your dad. Seriously? Is there anyway we can get in contact with him? I know he's on a mission or whatever, but Charlie, this is serious," Wiz said. "Everything points to the fact that we're dealing with something real, something dangerous. Those two nimrod classmates of ours are outside playing beanbag toss with a possessed fat boy!" Wiz paused for a second. I must've gone pale or looked sick or something. "Uh . . . are you okay?" he asked.

"We can't get ahold of my dad. We really can't."

"Really? Like there's no way? Like it's completely impossible?"

"Yeah. Totally impossible," I whispered.

"Okay," Wiz said quietly. "I don't want to talk to Cortez either, so maybe we can just stay here? What happens if we ride it out? What happens tomorrow morning? I have the ghost zapper and we're far away from the trails and from the cemetery. Let's just hide."

"Yeah. Yeah. Maybe," I said. "We all sleep in here, right?"

The walkie-talkie in my backpack came to life again. Someone said, "No way." We both heard it snap and pop like a radio in between stations.

"You think Cortez is listening?" Wiz asked.

"I can't turn the thing off, dude."

"We should throw it off a cliff," Wiz said.

Just then a blood-curdling scream pierced Gramps' workshop wall.

"Holy shit! Was that Mattheson?"

Wiz nodded. "We better check it out." He scooped up the ghost zapper thing that was hooked to a big battery. We bolted for the door.

CHAPTER EIGHTEEN

They'd just been playing beanbag toss out there in the yard. Beanbag is a pretty simple game. There are two wood ramps, each with a hole. One team tries to throw their beanbags through the hole in one ramp. The other team tries to throw their beanbag through the other ramp. Mouse and Mattheson hadn't ever played it, but came up with some rules. They decided that you got a point if your beanbag landed on the ramp at all. You got three points if you whipped your beanbag into the hole. They started shouting, "Corn hole!" when somebody managed to get the bag through the hole. For whatever reason, the ghost girl Paula, stuck in Riley's body, was amazing. She could whip the sack in the hole like fifty percent of the time. Shouting "Corn hole" stopped being that funny.

Because these dudes, Mouse and Mattheson, are both inventive as shit (all their life they'd been making up stupid games with each other) and also easily bored with any activity that didn't include the possibility of grave physical harm, pretty quickly they decided to alter the rules.

The Wisniewskis' backyard reaches deep into woods, to the side of a steep incline that's not buildable. They've got no neighbors directly behind them. They do have some badass landscape, though. In fact, the edge of their property is cut by a steep ravine, fifteen feet deep.

Mouse, Mattheson and Riley (Paula) carried the beanbag toss ramps into the darkness, away from Gramps' shack. There was just enough light from the rising moon to make out the trail in front of them. Within in a few moments, they came across the ravine.

"Dude!" Mouse shouted. "You know what?"

"Trans-canyon sack tossing!" Mattheson cried.

"That's a ravine. My old house was built on one," Paula said from Riley's face. If Mouse and Mattheson picked up on signs, they might've noticed Paula's nervousness at being on the ravine's edge. Mouse and Mattheson didn't notice shit.

"Ravine tossing!" Mattheson shouted.

Mattheson carried a ramp back through the woods, found a flat trail around the ravine's source, then crashed through brush and trees to position himself directly across the ravine from Mouse and Riley's body. There, he placed the beanbag ramp. "If you can corn hole this shit, you're God, dude!" Mattheson shouted across the ravine.

Riley/Paula, even though there was barely any light, even though the ghost girl twitched with fear in Riley's skin, launched the beanbag across the ravine, over a hundred feet, and sunk it square in the hole!

"Corn hole! Corn hole! Corn hole!" Mattheson screamed, jumping up and down, punching his fists into the air. And then he fell over the side of the ravine into the darkness below. He didn't cry out or anything. What Wiz and I heard in the cabin wasn't his fall. That came a moment later.

"Oh no. Oh shit. Mattheson? Mattheson!" Mouse screamed. He turned to Riley. "We have to go down there. We have to recover his dead body!"

Riley's body trembled, shook like a dry leaf. "He's not dead," Riley's face whispered. "But his soul will soon be devoured."

Right then Mattheson screamed like Mouse had never heard before. "What do you mean, bro? I mean, girl? Whatever!"

Riley spoke in monotone. "There are shadows in the tunnels and the fractured earth gives them rise. They will come further and further out from now until the break of day when a quaking will close the doorways again."

Mattheson screamed once more.

"I gotta go after him!" Mouse cried. He dropped, rolled onto his gut, dangled his legs over the side and began to slide down into the darkness.

A moment later, Wiz and I made it to where Riley/Paula stood, petrified, at the edge of the ravine.

"What's happening? What's going on?" I shouted.

"I'm very good at beanbag," Riley's face said.

"Where are Mouse and Mattheson, Paula?" Wiz asked.

Riley pointed into the ravine. "Getting their souls eaten. I'm sorry."

"Not good, dude. Not good!" I shouted.

Wiz was already sliding down the side of the ravine, holding on to the ghost zapper. I know he wasn't sure the zapper would even work. Total courage, pals! I jumped down on my ass and did the same thing, began to slide. As I went over the edge, I shouted up at Paula, "We wouldn't be in this mess without you barging into our lives, Paula Kelly! If there's anything human in you, better damn well help out right now!" Then down I slid.

The bottom of the ravine was muddy as shit, which was good, because it could've been rocky and deadly. As soon as I hit the ground, I backed myself against the wall. I listened hard, because I couldn't see anything in the darkness.

Someone was breathing near me. It whispered, "That you, Charlie?" It was Wiz.

"Yeah. Now what?" I whispered.

Something moved in the darkness, maybe thirty feet away.

"The zapper only can zap once with its battery. Otherwise, I'd zap and zap, man." Wiz's voice warbled. The dude was clearly scared out of his mind.

Luckily, we didn't have to wait long for something to happen. Mouse apparently had a lighter in his pants pocket. He lit it. "Bros?" he whispered.

"Over here!" I shouted.

Mouse ran towards the sound of our voices, the lighter still lit. There was the sound of wind buzzing through fabric, like lots of fabric, like shredded canvas or something. This deep darkness, more dark than the air, rose in a large, human form behind Mouse.

"Watch out!" Wiz cried.

"Behind you!" I cried.

Mouse turned and was enveloped in darkness. We heard a muffled scream. Then the darkness turned to flame. Fabric hissed, opened, revealing a loudly screaming Mouse. The thing, the Shadow, was on fire! It was bright enough to illuminate another Shadow being, which was perched on top of Mattheson's body in front of an opening to a cave. Mattheson struggled and kicked. His eyes landed on us. He screamed, "Help!"

I guess that's all Paula could take up there on the ravine's rim. She (in Riley's body) leapt from above, crying, "No!" into the night sky, and landed square on the back of the Shadow beast, which exploded into hundreds of fabric shreds that swirled into the air. Some of them caught fire in the flames licking off the other Shadow beast, which was still draped over screaming Mouse. The Shreds weren't nearly beaten though. The Shreds each had energy and intent of their own. They swarmed around Paula/Riley. They swarmed back over Mattheson. Both of our dudes screamed and kicked and punched.

"Got to do it," Wiz said. He pushed himself off the ravine wall and ran into the center of the fray, ghost zapper held high. "Please! Work!" he screamed.

Suddenly there was a flash of purple light, a crackling noise, then what sounded like a sonic boom, hot wind, and flames everywhere that knocked me off my feet, and then a shocking, total darkness. Everything was silent for a few moments and then I heard a moan.

"I lost my energy. I need a cheeseburger," Paula/Riley's voice said.

Mouse lit his lighter again. He was completely covered in soot, but the Shadow and the Shreds were gone. "Did we win?" he asked.

"I think so," I said. "Wiz? Are you out there?"

The figure of Wiz pushed itself off the ground. "Yeah. I think I flew up in the air . . . but the Zapper worked, didn't it?"

"It really did, man," I said.

Mouse's lighter went out for a moment. He flicked it back on. "Lighter is hot, bros. Can't keep it on." He moved his arm and illuminated Riley and Mattheson's groaning bodies. "You guys alive?"

"Yeah?" Mattheson said.

"No energy," Riley's head said.

"Shit! Can't do it anymore!" Mouse said. "Burning thumb!"

The light extinguished. I heard the lighter drop onto the ground nearby.

"Does anyone's phone have a charge?" I asked into the dark.

Everyone who had one tried, but the phones would not work.

"We might have to wait until morning to get out of here," I said.

"He'll come here. He'll shred me here. We're at a tunnel opening. I'll be ripped to a thousand pieces. Or you will be, Charlie Wilkins. We have to leave," Paula whimpered.

Tunnels. I thought of the tracing paper in the guest-book. Dad had a collection of old maps. A couple of them had what he called a "vellum overlay." There was one that showed underground stuff. You put the overlay on the regular mountain map, and you could see where the caves lay beneath the mountains. Could the tracing paper contain maps of tunnels?

"There's a tunnel opening in the ravine?" I asked.

"Yes, Charlie Wilkins," Riley's mouth said.

Then I tried to climb up the ravine wall, but slid right back down. "Where does the ravine end?" I asked Wiz.

"At a cliff," Wiz replied. "We're screwed. We have to wait until someone notices we're gone."

Fear rose up around me in the dark. A cliff on one end? A tunnel opening on the other? Shredded? Riley? And what about my connection to Paula? Would I be shredded, too? What would these Shadow things do to Mouse, Mattheson and Wiz? "We have to do something," I said. "Riley, can you move?"

"Maybe. So tired," Riley's face said.

"Can you come over here and get down on all fours? What if we build a tower? If we put Riley on the bottom, Mattheson on top of him, me on top of Mattheson, then

Wiz and then Mouse, maybe Mouse can climb out, run back to the workshop and get a ladder."

"That might work," Wiz said.

Just then someone shouted from near the ravine's rim, "Wizard? You out here?"

"Oh man! Gramps!" Wiz cried.

We all stood together, gathered. A moment later, the beam of a strong flashlight landed on our faces.

"Gramps!" Wiz cried again.

Wiz's grandpa knew all about the ravine, of course, and when he heard screaming coming from the woods behind the workshop, he'd grabbed his flashlight and a rope ladder he'd carried with him in Vietnam.

As I climbed up, the last in the crew to get out of the ravine, he shined the flashlight in my face. "Hello," I said, quietly.

Then he shined the light across the other faces. Mouse and Mattheson were totally covered in soot. Riley looked like the walking dead. "Now what happened, Wizard? Why did you guys have that bug zapper down in the ravine?"

"Well . . . we meant to just play beanbag toss. That's why the targets are out on either side."

"And you did this in the dark?" Gramps said.

"Uh huh. And then I accidentally threw a bag in the ravine, but we couldn't find it, so we all went down there, and I . . . I thought the bug zapper was a lantern, so that's why I had it out here with me . . ."

"And you all went down into the ravine without a way to get back out, because none of you are smart enough to consider the consequences of such a goddamn stupid act as that?" Gramps said.

"Yeah," Wiz said.

"Just because you have friends doesn't mean you gotta turn into a damn idiot." Gramps trudged into the woods, back toward the house.

We began to follow. "I think the tracing paper are map overlays, maybe tunnels," I whispered to Wiz.

"Yeah, no kidding, Sherlock Holmes," Wiz whispered back. "We're in deep shit. We have to contact Cortez immediately."

"Okay," I said. We really didn't have any other options, did we?

CHAPTER NINETEEN

Mouse and Mattheson hung back as we made our way to Gramps' workshop. I didn't know it at the time, but the truth is, we nearly lost them. And why wouldn't we? Who in their right minds would stick around after getting draped with ghost rags that caught fire and blew up in a purple light? Riley had a ghost inside him, so he had to go along for the ride. I was somehow connected to this ghost, right? I had to go along, too. Wiz had turned from total skeptic to a dude living out the dreams of one of the fantasy novels he loved and he was keeping himself out of military school by hanging with kids his own age. But what did Mouse and Mattheson have to gain from this shit?

Terror? Pain? Death? Even for a couple of dudes who enjoyed the death-defying in their skating life, death by Shadow couldn't seem too attractive. At least not to Mouse.

"As soon as we get back to the house, we duck and run, bro. Get our boards and get the hell out, okay?" Mouse whispered.

"Why?" Mattheson asked. "Maybe the old man will cook us some food or something."

"Did you fall into that ravine, dude?" Mouse asked. "You didn't just lose your balance, right?"

"No. I got sucked in. I wouldn't just fall over, bro."

"See! I knew it. You got attacked and then we both nearly got fudge balled by a couple of giant rag demons, dude," Mouse said. "And my question to you is why?"

"Because . . ." Mattheson couldn't get another word out.

"Because we're hanging out with possessed fat boys and demon explorers and nerd boys. If we're by ourselves, do we ever get attacked?" Mouse said.

"Yeah, by the girl," Mattheson said. "The ghost girl. Down on Highway 101."

"That was an accident," Mouse said. "She wasn't looking for us. She even said so! I say we leave and go make some damn pizza rolls, and keep our asses safe."

"I don't know," Mattheson said. "Let's at least stay for a little bit and see if there's any food here. Riley's got to eat something or the girl will die."

"She's already dead, bro!" Mouse said.

"You know what I mean," Mattheson said.

By that time, we'd all made it back to Gramps' shack. Gramps told us he was at a good part in the movie he was watching and we better keep it down and we better not go outside in the dark like a bunch of dumbass fools. Wiz promised we'd stay put. Gramps went upstairs to his living quarters and we all gathered around the table, including Mouse and Mattheson.

Riley's head lolled around on his neck. His eyes rolled back. "Argh . . ." Paula said.

"I zapped her. The bug zap thing might have destroyed her if she weren't wrapped in Riley. What can we do to get your energy back up, Paula?"

"Cheeseburger," Riley's mouth whispered.

"See?" Mattheson said. "Food."

"Shut up," Mouse said.

Suddenly Riley's eyes shot open. He sat bolt upright. He (Paula) looked Mouse square in the face. "Please don't leave me, little skater boy," she said. "I came to you for an important reason. I need you. Please!" Riley's eyes blinked. A tear fell down his face. Then he deflated again.

Mouse stared at Riley. He could see the ghost girl inside him, the beautiful, terrifying nerd girl from down on Highway 101. "Aw shit," Mouse said.

"Please?" she asked.

"Fine. I'm not . . . I'm not going anywhere," Mouse mumbled. "Not for now."

"He wants to, though," Mattheson said, "But I said we have to wait for food."

"Please don't go, Mouse," Paula whispered.

"Okay," Mouse said. Nobody had really needed Mouse before, so this was a pretty huge deal to him. He sat up straight and put his hand over his heart. "I promise I won't go, nerd girl."

Wiz stood up. "Gramps made rice crispy bars yesterday. I'll get them. You get ahold of Cortez, Charlie."

CHAPTER TWENTY

There was a snap and a pop, the sound of a radio between stations. I'd carried the guest book and the walkie-talkie outside of Gramps' workshop, so I wouldn't have any trouble hearing (also I didn't want to scare the dudes inside, if Cortez said something crazy). Before I could even say anything, the walkie-talkie spoke. "You finally doing something, little guy? You finally get that you're all meat without me?"

I pressed the talk button and said, "Is this Cortez?"

"Oh, yeah. No kidding, Charlie. Of course it is. I gave you the walkie-talkie, didn't I? I've been talking at you through it, haven't I? Who the heck else would it be?"

"Well . . . Can you come help us? We're ready."

"Little too late," Cortez said. "I'm in final preparations myself. Tick-tock. Gotta be ready. You want help, you bring that book out to me."

"To where?" I asked.

"Page 78. Red dot. It's almost 9, kid. Eight hours from now and we'll be toast. Get on it!"

"Wait. Cortez?" I said.

The radio popped and snapped.

"Shit! Cortez!" I shouted.

Cortez didn't respond.

I propped the guest book on a stump and turned to page 78 (there were numbers written, not typed, on the upper-outside corners of the pages). There, I found an entire map of Encinitas and surrounding areas. The red dot was in east Poway, right backed up against a mountain and scrub lands. It had to be at least thirty miles away! How the hell were we supposed to get there?

Suddenly the walkie-talkie sprang to life again. "Ask the fat boy if he can drive. Ha ha. Bet he can."

Before I went in, I pulled some of the tracing paper (the "vellum overlays") out from the back of the book. I put several of the papers over the map. One seemed to fit well. I turned it around and lined it up to the edges of the map. And then I saw it, in small print at the bottom, somebody—I think my dad, based on the handwriting— had scrawled, "Match to 78." Yeah, page 78. I'd definitely found the right overlay for the map.

I wasn't yet entirely sure that the network of lines on the paper had anything to do with the tunnels; I sort of fig- ured, though, and Wiz had come to the same conclusion, too, right? I traced one of the lines right across an area on the map that was probably Wiz's backyard, probably the ravine. I also saw that two tunnels ran out towards Poway and Cortez. There were two places where a bunch of tunnels came together. One was the Whaley House in San Diego (green dot and labeled on the map). The other was right on the edge between Natural Trails and Olivenhain Cemetery (black dot, no label). That's where our stuff got buried. That's where Rooster boy attacked me and Wiz. I nodded. "Okay. This is right," I said. Then I closed the book and went inside.

Riley was back upright sitting at the table, sort of bouncing on his ass (all of them were sitting on wooden stools). The energy that had been throbbing through him almost constantly since his possession had clearly returned. Guess the rice crispy treats did the trick.

Weirdly, Mattheson was in the same state. All happy and jumpy. Sugar apparently had the same affect on him as it did possessed boys. They all looked up at me like they expected news, which I had. It just wasn't good news.

"Is Cortez going to meet us some place?" Wiz asked.

"No. We have to go to him."

Wiz seemed immediately skeptical. "Where?"

"East Poway. By a mountain," I said.

"We can't do that!" Wiz said. "That's so far. You want to double ride me on your bike?"

"Riley? Paula? Do you know how to drive?" I asked.

Riley's head lit up like a smiling pumpkin. "I'm a great driver. I just got my license!" Riley's face said.

Why would Cortez know that, I wondered?

"Dude, you're in eighth grade," Mouse said.

"I am not. I'm a sophomore!" Riley's face shouted.

"How come you're in our science class, then!" Mattheson barked.

"You're talking to Paula Kelly, not Riley, remember?" I said. I pulled the newspaper article out of the book. Mouse, Mattheson and Riley stared down at it, at the picture of Paula Kelly smiling. The article detailed Paula's grisly murder.

"That is you," Mouse whispered. "So hot."

"That is me," Riley said. "Rooster killed me when the earth shook hard and the energy was released and he had the power, but he couldn't take my soul and so I slid from tunnel to tunnel, always on the run so I wouldn't be made into Shreds. But now the energy is back and soon it's going to be . . . going to be . . . and I'm going to be . . ." Riley's face turned red and he started to sob. "Yankee Jim won't stop until my soul is in pieces that can't ever be together again that fly around screaming forever, clumping up in those big shadows!"

"Is what attacked us in the ravine, the rag beings are clumps of souls?" Wiz asked.

"Yes, yes," Paula said.

"Yankee Jim?" I asked. There was that bastard's name again! "I thought Rooster killed you."

"Don't say his name!" Paula cried. "Please!"

I wanted to ask more about Yankee right then, but Riley shook. You could totally see and feel Paula Kelly, murdered girl, crying inside him. It was sick. It was not good. It made my chest hurt.

"Aw shit. I didn't mean to upset you," I said.

"We won't let anything happen to you," Wiz said. Seeing Paula like that must've hurt Wiz, too.

Mouse stood up from his stool and gave Riley a big hug. "It's okay, girl," he said. "We'll keep you safe." Yeah, and Mouse.

Wiz leaned over to me. "As soon as Gramps is asleep, we can take his truck out to see Cortez," Wiz whispered.

"Okay," I said.

Not more than a half-hour later we could all hear snores rattling the floorboards above us.

"That is gnarly, bro," Mattheson said looking up at the ceiling.

"Deviated septum. Pretty gross," Wiz said. Then Wiz crept up the stairs and was gone for about a minute. When he returned, he carried Gramps' keys.

"He's asleep," Wiz whispered. "I guess it's time." Wiz pulled the guest book from my hand, opened it on the table, ripped the map out from between pages 77 and 79 and then he turned to leave.

"Wait. You're not bringing the guest book?" I asked.

Wiz turned back to us. "No. Cortez really wants it. If we take it to him, he'll have what he needs, right? Maybe he won't help us, then. Why would he? Just to be nice? We need to know where we're safe, where we're in danger, what kinds of things might attack us, when the threat is at its worst and when it will end, if it will end. I think he has this information. I think he knows what your dad would know. But we may need to pressure him. We know he wants the book. We keep the book from him, we keep the power."

We all stood in silence for a moment. "Damn, dude. That's sick," I said. "So good."

"See?" Mattheson whispered. "Wizzy is so smart."

I found out later that Wiz lifted that speech pretty much straight out of one of his favorite steampunk novels, including the shit about *he knows what your dad would know*. Guess it's good to read. I wish he'd thought to bring the Magrath Stock Shock and the bug zapper, though. Weapons would've been helpful at a certain point.

Yeah. We could've used some badass steampunk weapons.

CHAPTER TWENTY-ONE

One by one, we slid out of the work door into the night and tiptoed down the trail to the driveway where Gramps parked the truck. Along the way, an owl hooted, which made Riley/Paula jump about five feet off the ground, which made Mattheson laugh, which made me say, "Shut up, dude."

We emerged from the woods and Wiz's head dropped. "Mom parked right behind him," he whispered. Behind Gramps' 70s-era blue and white Ford sat the brand new Lexus SUV.

"I can drive through the grass," Riley/Paula said. "There's plenty of room to cruise on by. This is going to be great."

"You sure?" Wiz asked.

Riley/Paula nodded. Wiz handed over the keys.

"There's not enough room up front. Somebody's going to have to ride in the bed," I said. "I'll go in back, but somebody else will have to, too."

Mouse and Mattheson both leapt into the back and lay down. I followed. I slid as far front as I could and looked in the cab's window.

Inside the cab, Riley smiled like a pumpkin. Paula Kelly was pretty psyched to drive, apparently. It had been thirty-five years of not being able to. Riley's hand stuck the key in and turned the ignition. The truck roared to life.

"Shit. Can you be more quiet?" Wiz shouted.

"What?" Riley cried. He threw it into gear, popped the clutch and the truck leapt forward. He spun the wheel and we ripped to the right nearly crashing into a stand of scrubby pine. I screamed. Wiz's face smacked against the window. In back, Mouse, Mattheson and I all crashed together then flew to the other side of the bed, smashing flat like pancakes. Riley/Paula righted the truck and it bounced over the lawn and out on to the street, spraying sparks as the back hit curb. And then we were off, barreling down the road in the wrong direction.

"This is a bad idea," Wiz said, wincing and rubbing his head.

"I love to drive!" Paula cried from inside Riley.

For about thirty minutes we rolled east into hills and then from the coastal region into scrub and mountains east of Poway. There was very little traffic on the road and the stars were huge, like freaking fat, above us. Other than the ridiculous speed with which Paula took corners (always throwing us in the back against the truck's rail—we totally cried in protest and pain, but it didn't do any good), she did pretty well. She (using Riley's hands) worked the truck across its gears really smoothly.

When we weren't being smashed, I was staring through the cab's window. The entire way, Wiz held his flashlight over the map and directed. Finally, the truck rounded a corner and Wiz shouted, "Here, here! I think? Go right!"

Paula took a right off the road. The truck bounced along this pitted drive that jarred the dudes up front, but absolutely smashed those of us in the bed, especially Mouse, who is light as a damn feather. He caught three feet of air during one particularly bad bump. I had to reach out and grab Mouse's t-shirt to keep him from flying off like a kite.

"That was rad, bro," Mouse shouted into the air.

"You have to slow down, Riley . . . I mean Paula," Wiz shouted. "You want to kill everybody?"

"Mellow out, Wizzy," Paula said with Riley's big mouth.

About a mile in, we came to a small ridge that overlooked a great moonlit stretch of rock and scrub on one side and a mountain on the other. It looked painted. All dark orange and green bush barely lit, opening up into an ocean of sky and space. Shit. Damn amazing. Riley/Paula let the truck roll to a halt. Mouse, Mattheson and I all stood up and looked over the roof of the cab. "Is that real, what we're seeing?" Riley/Paula asked.

I'm a realist though, pals. "We're about to roll into a bunch of scorpions and coyotes," I said.

"According to the map we should be here," Wiz said. He shined the flashlight out the window. "There are some mailboxes on the right. Maybe one is Cortez's?"

Three mailboxes stood on posts at the side of the road. Riley put the truck in gear and pulled up. Wiz leaned out and shined his flashlight on the boxes. The one furthest on the right had no address number on it, but did have H. Cortez written on its side in big, block letters.

"Okay. This is it," Wiz said.

A few moments later, we were out of the truck and on foot. I walked side by side with Wiz up a narrow, dirt path between boulders and shrubs. As we moved along this rise, heading toward a mountain, the fat stars hanging above us, I took a deep breath. Something about the experience, being with these dudes, off our school grounds, having been driven there by a possessed fourteen-year-old, made me feel connected to Dad, and not just because the adventure was like something he might've been on himself at some point. It was bigger. I couldn't tell you why, exactly, but the trip to Cortez, the haunting of Riley, the paranormal attacks we'd endured just felt connected to Dad's disappearance.

The thought I might be able to save Dad slid through my mind.

And then I looked over at spindly Wiz walking next to me. I turned back to Mouse and Mattheson, both of the dudes totally wide-eyed in the moonlight. I turned in time to see Riley bend over a bush with sharp leaves, poke at it and pull his hand away quickly, like Paula forgot how thorns worked. Really, I had no idea why these guys were with me. Why were we together? What we were doing wasn't just a school project. Man, I just suddenly liked them all a lot.

We rounded a tall pile of rocks and came into view of a weird, like Western movie lean-to with light pouring out of every window. I stopped and put out my arms, holding the others from going any further. Cortez gave off a bad vibe. That's all I can say. A dog barked inside. A man—it was Cortez, of course—spoke loudly, "Did the boy finally find his way out here, dog?" The dog barked some more. "About time! Ha ha!"

"Boy? I think he must be talking about me, huh?" I said.

A moment later, a large Klieg light lit up a circle of desert in front of the lean-to. Cortez exited through the front door. His gray bush of an afro fired off his head and the giant bush of his white beard exploded from his face. He sort of looked nuts.

"Oh yeah, that dude," Mattheson mumbled. "I saw him down on Highway 101 right before Paula showed up there."

"He was at the coffee shop!" Mouse said.

Cortez wore an SDSU hoodie that pulled awkwardly across his big gut. He had crinkling, smiling eyes. His face was shiny, like it was coated in grease. "Hello. Yes, like the tunnels said. You're all here! Welcome, little dudes!" he called. "Come on in! I'll get you some drinks!" The little mangy dog barked some more. He pointed his big finger in the dog's face, which made the dog shut up. He turned and re-entered the shack, the dog right on his heels.

I looked at Wiz. "Like the tunnels said?"

"Don't want to stay long. Let's get our info, make a plan to meet him with the book if his info is true, then get the crap out," Wiz whispered.

I nodded. We both took big breaths and walked toward the door. The others followed behind. One by one, we entered the lean-to.

Inside, a fire roared in a fireplace in one corner. The dog seemed to have disappeared. It was hot as shit in there. The center of the room was totally dominated by a giant, heavy timber picnic table. One end of the table contained lit candles in a star pattern and a bunch of oils in different, little glass containers.

"Don't mind the shrine. I'm in the middle of anointing my bod, buddies, to keep them spirits from squeezing into me later tonight. I'm a sponge," Cortez called over his shoulder, as he reached into his refrigerator.

A shelf against the back wall (which seemed to be made entirely of multi-colored Indian beads) contained dozens more lit candles next to dozens of skeleton figurines. All the skeletons were doing different, totally undead activities (dancing, motorcycle riding, newspaper reading, rifle shooting, skeleton sex, etc.).

"Dope skeletons, dude," Mouse said.

"Thank you, friend!" Cortez said. He poured red liquid into glasses on the counter.

Near where Cortez poured drinks stood a giant suit of, like, real Spanish armor on a small, round platform.

"Sit down, little dudes!" Cortez called over his shoulder.

Mouse and Mattheson made their way to the table and sat down. Riley/Paula dicked around, moving from the knickknack shelves to a couple of waist high statues of goats. He touched and sniffed everything. He bent over and put his damn tongue on one goat. I shit you not.

Me, I hung back. I almost couldn't move. Wiz seemed to be in the same position as me. Glued in place.

As Riley/Paula got close to Cortez, Riley flinched, craned his neck and stared at Cortez. Cortez nodded and smiled. "I'm not the only sponge in the room, am I? Another one of us is good at taking in the spirits, am I right?"

Riley's face got red. Then I remembered it was Cortez who suggested Riley drive. Did Cortez know about Riley's possession? Did he know Paula had somehow stashed herself in the boy? Ghost demon boy Rooster had said, "*Don't save the girl . . .*" Did Cortez know we were protecting the girl, even though we hadn't tried? The short hairs rose on the back of my neck. I decided I better sit down or I'd give away my nerves.

Wiz completely refused to sit. He shifted his weight back and forth, eyeballs locked on the side of Cortez's head. "Hey, we have some questions," Wiz said.

Cortez turned and smiled. "Slow down buddy. Sit! Relax!" He then placed the red "juices" on a tray and made his way over to the table. He placed a glass in front of each of us. "Rose hip tea. Already steeped and sweetened, boys!" He handed a glass to Wiz who stayed standing. While Cortez was turned away from us for a second, putting the tray back on the counter, I tried to gesture not to drink the shit, but Mouse and Mattheson didn't see me. They started sipping and making barf faces right away. Turns out it wasn't poisoned, thankfully. Just butt-ass bad.

Cortez then slid onto the bench across from me. His gut pressed up against the table and tipped the bench back a bit so Mouse and Mattheson, who were both next to him, also leaned back. "Ha ha! I'm too large for this table! I don't know why I would buy such a godawful small table!" Then he leveled a stare at Riley next to me. His lip curled up and he almost whispered, "How are you, sweetie?"

At first, Riley/Paula didn't answer. Riley's face flushed. Finally, Riley's mouth mumbled, "I think I'm okay."

"Are you?" Cortez said. He turned back to me. "So, I imagine you've been getting chased around a little by now, Charlie Wilkins? Did the ghoulies give you any more warning? Did they steal any of your stuff?"

"They took things from everybody," I said. "My bike."

"My underpants, dude!" Mattheson said.

"Hey, I've got Riley's . . ." Mouse pulled the messed up Han Solo out of his pocket. Is this Riley's?" Mouse handed the action figure to Paula who stared at it.

"I think he says yes," Riley's mouth said.

Cortez winked at Riley. He laughed. "The ghoulies got energy right now. They can move from where they died, out of the earth away from home at the moment. It's going to get hella worse, little pals. Especially now that you're protecting that chica, huh?"

I swallowed hard. Cortez knew about Paula, no doubt. I mumbled, "Some black rag things got close to us a couple hours ago. But we managed to destroy them with a reverse bug zapper Wiz made."

"Nice! Reverse bug zapper. That's genius, nerd boy!" Cortez said.

"Do you know what we're talking about?" Wiz asked. "The rag beings?"

"Sure. Shadows," Cortez said. "Scary beasts, ain't they? Not controlled by a central processor, either."

"No brains?" Wiz asked.

"Nope. They're conglomerates of shredded, Trembler souls, nerd boy."

"That's what Paula said!" Mattheson shouted.

I glared at him, but it really didn't matter if we said Paula's name.

"When Tremblers are whole they move around with purpose, with a 'brain' I guess, if you want to call it that. They ain't too smart, though. They don't know they're dead so they don't cross over into the light."

"And what's a Trembler?" Wiz asked.

"Normal ghost. Paula Kelly?" Cortez smiled wide at Riley. "She's a Trembler."

"I'm not dead! I'm in Riley!" Riley's face said.

"See what I mean?" Cortez said, laughing and winking.

"Wait, I got murdered!" Riley shouted.

"Good for you, Paula! Dose of reality!" Cortez said. "Anyhoo, the Tremblers aren't to be confused with ghosts. Tremblers won't hurt yuh. But the Hungry? Those suckers know they're dead but they don't cross over into the light either. And they don't for one reason only: so they can get revenge in this dimension. Those things are starving for revenge and the best revenge a Hungry ghost can get is shredding the soul of someone he hates."

"Shredding!" Riley's face cried.

"Yeah, girl," Cortez said quietly. "Shredding pretty much sends the soul to hell on earth, doesn't it?"

"Yes," Riley's face squeaked out.

Cortez looked back to me. "What happens is lots of Shreds, trying to get whole, mash up, clump together, become these rag beings as the nerd boy called them. We call them Shadows, and the bastards sure do suck. Since they got no minds of their own, Hungry ones can control them." Cortez smiled big and friendly. Then he said, "Say, you got past your dad's cloaking bird, I take it! Let's take a look at that guest book! Where is it?"

"Is that boy Rooster a Hungry ghost?" I asked.

"Yup. He got run over by a rich dude in a speeding Mercer. In 1922, I believe. Kid is mad as shit and is from a family of crazy bastards who all want revenge." Cortez smiled at me. "So where's the book?" he asked.

"So, that Rooster boy wants revenge on Paula Kelly? He wants to shred her?" Wiz asked.

"Right. You got the book here, Charlie?" Cortez asked.

"But why does he want me? Why do I have anything to do with Rooster? If he doesn't shred Paula he wants me instead? I'm mean, I'm not even a ghost!" I said.

"Where the hell is that goddamn book?" Cortez growled.

Mouse spun off the bench and stood. "Hey, chill, hippie," he said. "Don't get all monkey ass on my posse."

"We forgot the book. But we want to give it to you," Wiz said. "Seriously. It was a mistake."

"Why do you want it, anyway?" I said.

"Because it's mine, you bitch!" Cortez cried. He pounded his fists into the table. The glasses of red tea, rose hip or whatever, all spilled.

I spun and stood up off the bench. So did Mattheson.

"And now all hell's gonna break loose and my guest book, all me and my family's hard work, ain't gonna matter anymore!" Red tea began to run off the sides of the table.

I stood next to Wiz. Mouse and Mattheson slid around the table and lined up next to us. Only Riley stayed seated, right across from Cortez. "We will get you the book in time, okay?" Wiz said. "But you have to help us. How can we stop Rooster? We won't allow Paula Kelly to be shredded and we won't allow a hair on Charlie Wilkins' head to be harmed."

"Yeah, bitch!" Mattheson shouted.

"Not one hair on Charlie Wilkins' head," Riley's face hissed. Riley's hand reached across the table and grabbed the front of Cortez's sweatshirt, "Do you understand, hippie?"

Cortez glared straight at Paula in Riley. Then his eyes crinkled and he began to laugh like Santa Claus. "You're a team, hey? Good for you!"

Riley's hand released Cortez slowly. Riley's body kicked back the bench and it stood up then stepped back to fall in line with the rest of us.

Cortez's dog bolted out from behind a cupboard and started barking.

Cortez shook his head and kept laughing. "Jesus B. Christmas, you dumb shits. You're standing there acting all big and tough, but it don't matter."

"What doesn't?" Wiz asked.

"Your team, because you don't got time. At dawn a quake is going to hit this region. A big one. The energy is already shooting around in the crust below us as we speak. The Hungry ones, like Rooster, the Shadows, they're getting bigger and stronger right now. That's why your fat turd of a friend is capable of grabbing me like an ape. That's why he's capable of jumping up on buildings. Paula Kelly is thick with quake energy. She's not the only one, boys. The ghoulies are only going to get bigger, tougher and meaner tonight. And when that quake hits at sun up, while all that pent up energy is being released, they'll be powerful enough to cut your flesh right off your bones and snatch your souls right from inside of you."

"Shit!" Mouse shouted.

"That's right, shit. No bug zapper is going to work on a hyper-charged Hungry Ghost!" Cortez stared at us and nodded, maybe to let it sink in that our weapons weren't going to work against Rooster. Then he spoke again. "Now if you can capture Rooster before the quake, you might be able to save Paula and this fat ass kid she decided to invade. You bring me the book at 4 a.m. at the Olivenhain Cottage and I'll help you. I'll guarantee you get Rooster. Can you do that, Charlie Wilkins? Can you be a better man than your old man was? Can you make *and* keep a promise?"

Then it was my turn to pound my fist into the table. It was freaking immediate. I didn't stop to think. The power of my punch shook the whole damn lean-to. "You shut up about my dad," I hissed. Man, I didn't even know what he was talking about, but it sure made me homicidal.

The dog growled at me. Without looking down, Cortez pointed his finger and the dog whimpered and ran back behind the cupboard.

Cortez smirked. "Hot tempered, huh, Wilkins?" Then he turned to Wiz. "Nerd boy. Sit down a second. I need you to make a list of items to bring to the Olivenhain Cottage with you. If Charlie acts like a man and brings my book, we'll build ourselves a Rooster trap, because trapping is the only way the sucker will lay off."

Wiz paused for a second. Thought. Then, he nodded and moved over to the table. Cortez started speaking to him in whispers.

"Why'd you schiz, bro? What's up with your dad?" Mouse asked me.

"Nothing. This asshole knows nothing at all."

A few seconds later Wiz stood and came back over to us.

Cortez leaned forward. "You got almost no time, little dudes. You got Shadows gunning for you and they're getting stronger by the minute. If you don't catch Rooster before dawn, he will get Paula, and if he can't do that, Charlie Wilkins is the one who will pay. Death and dismemberment, boys! Now go get me my damn book or there's going to be blood!"

CHAPTER TWENTY-TWO

I don't know if we even had time to think. I can't remember being scared.

I do remember running, though. I do remember Cortez's dog barking. Wiz went out the door first, ran ahead on the path outside Cortez's house. Even though he's not a streak of lightning by any means, we all struggled to keep up with him.

"What the hell, Wizzy? I've never seen you move so fast," Mouse shouted.

"Paula," Wiz said to Riley when we got back to the truck. "Drive fast, okay?"

"Yes, Wizard," Riley's face said.

"Why does ghost boy Rooster only care about Paula and Charlie?" Mattheson asked, climbing into the back of the truck. "What, aren't we dope enough?"

I was about to jump in back, but Wiz shouted, "Charlie, up front. We need to talk on the drive."

"Yeah. Right. Good," I said. I climbed in the cab next to Wiz. I could totally see Riley's body trembling. "You okay, dude?"

"I have to drive fast," Paula said using Riley's mouth.

"Yeah. So, go," Wiz said.

Riley's hand turned the key in the ignition, jammed the truck into gear and popped the clutch. The truck leapt forward then skidded through gravel and sand, turning us around to head back to Encinitas, back toward a shitty little ghost boy, a Hungry little bitch named Rooster (and his minion of scary-ass Shadows).

That's a shit lot for a crew of damn eighth graders to deal with!

As the truck sped through the night, wind whipping into its open windows, Wiz shouted in my ear. "Cortez gave me a list of materials to bring to build a trap, but he must think I'm stupid. I know what that list of junk makes. It's a solar energy collector, with some adjustments. I can build it. We don't need that hippie at all!"

"But, he's got experience with this stuff," I shouted over the wind. "I know he's an asshole, but it's going to be like one in the morning before we're home. Do we have time? Maybe we need him?"

"Dude. He's not interested in Paula's well being. He just wants the guest book."

"Do you feel something weird?" I asked.

"What?" Wiz asked.

I gripped the door. Something trembled. Seriously. It wasn't the truck. It came from below the truck, like below the road's surface, like the Earth's crust strained and shifted, which sent vibrations and heat into cracks, into the tunnels. I felt it. Sensed it. I didn't hear it, but you know what? Paula did. A great *ah* rose from the ghosts and shadows below us, as they absorbed the energy released.

"Oh! Did you hear that?" Riley's face cried. "Fight or flight?"

We turned to look at Riley. His hair stood straight up. His face went pale and sweat beaded up on him.

"What? What's going down, Paula?" I asked.

Riley face didn't respond. Instead, his foot pressed the gas pedal to the floor and the truck shot forward, jumping from fifty to seventy miles per hour in a flash.

"Shit!" I shouted. I turned and looked back into the truck bed, where the wind crushed Mouse and Mattheson. They tried to stay low, but every bump in the road launched them up into the wicked wind, which blasted them back into the truck's closed gate.

"Ahhh!" Mattheson shouted.

"Slow the hell down!" Mouse cried.

"Paula! Serious!" I shouted.

But the truck sped into Encinitas. Below the road the Earth's crust again creaked, strained, released a little burst of vibration and heat. I felt it, heard it, and clearly Paula heard the *ah* rise from the shadows and ghosts.

"Oh God! Oh shit!" Riley's face cried. He turned sharp, so Mouse and Mattheson smashed to the side (Wiz's forehead smacked into my cheek). "This is happening!" Riley cried. "Fight or flight? Fight or flight?"

I had to act, pals. I unbuckled my seatbelt and leapt up onto Wiz's lap (Wiz screamed). I grabbed the wheel and tried to kick the gear shift with one foot and kick Riley's foot off the accelerator with the other.

"Flight!" Riley cried. He head-butted me in the cheek (right where Wiz's head had just hit!) then shoved the shit out of me with his elbow (and Paula was quake-power huge!), which totally knocked me off Wiz and smashed me into the side of the truck. For a moment, Riley lost control and we ran half off the road and pulverized a small palm tree.

"Holy shit!" Mouse cried from behind. He bounced high out of the truck bed. He landed on top of the gate, clung there like a monkey.

The truck skidded around a curve, nearly hit an old man taking a midnight bike ride. We all screamed.

"Paula! You've got to stop the truck!" I shouted.

"Flight!" Paula screamed.

Wiz was frozen. It was all up to me. I went after Riley again. I leapt onto Wiz, reared back like an ape-man and punched Riley in the temple.

"Don't!" Riley/Paula screamed.

"Stop the truck!" I screamed back.

Riley whipped the truck around a corner and headed into the heart of a residential neighborhood. Tears streamed down his face. We flew at a fork in the road.

"Turn, turn, turn," Wiz mumbled.

I yanked the wheel right and we barely made the fork, glancing off a tall hedge to the left.

"Stop!" I cried again. I reared back and monkey punched poor Riley. The punch landed on the side of his nose. Blood began to pour out.

Riley turned towards me. The terror in Paula exploded from of his eyes. "Flight!" he screamed. Then in one swift move, Paula unbuckled Riley and shouldered open the door. He dove out onto the street while the truck barreled on.

"Holy crap!" Wiz shouted.

Mouse and Mattheson saw his body roll past. They slid to the gate on their knees. "What the shit, Riley?" Mouse screamed.

They saw Riley/Paula push himself up and take off running down into a wooded yard.

Back in the cab, I jumped into the driver's seat and slammed on the brakes. The truck skidded up into a yard and stopped a foot shy of someone's ornate, concrete birdbath.

"Whoa," I whispered.

Wiz sat trembling, blinking, mouth hanging open. "Shit, shit, shit," he said. "We're not dead. We're not dead."

"Yeah. Not yet," I said. I jumped out of the truck and ran towards where Riley disappeared. Mouse and Mattheson leapt over the gate and followed.

"Riley! Paula!" I shouted into the woods. "It's okay. We're not mad. Whatever's happening to you, we just want to help. Come back!"

"Come back, bro!" Mouse shouted. "I mean, Paula!"
Mattheson shouted, too.

Wiz called from the truck. "Maybe we should split up, Charlie. Let's go to my place and get the stuff to build the trap."

"Okay!" I called. "Dudes, keep looking. I'm going to try to drive the truck over to Wiz's to get shit. We'll swing back past here in like fifteen," I said.

"Okay," Mouse said.

"This is some sick shit, bro," Mattheson said.

Back at the truck, Wiz was still breathing hard. I climbed the fuck in, turned the ignition, but the engine wouldn't start. "Shit," I said. Truth is, I had no idea how to drive a car. I'd never come close.

Wiz exhaled. Then he said, quietly, "Get out. I can drive this. I've driven manual drive lawnmowers before, anyway."

"Okay," I said.

A moment later, Wiz drove us down the street, the truck stalling and starting, but moving in the right direction to get back to his house. Something in my chest just sank, though.

We'd left Paula and Riley behind. We'd left Mouse and Mattheson.

CHAPTER TWENTY-THREE

I don't think we could've protected Paula at that point, though. Not without the Stock Shock and the more serious Shred-burning bug zapper, both of which we'd failed to take with us.

Riley told us the story of what happened a couple weeks later. He and Paula could communicate clearly by that point. They ran from the truck. Riley couldn't do anything about it.

What are we doing? he asked. *What are we doing? Ow. My arm hurts. We're bleeding. Paula, where are you going?*

She kept repeating, "Flight. Flight. Flight." It was probably from something she'd learned in school way back when, right? When under extreme pressure we have this physiological reaction to either kick ass or run the hell away? Paula was in flight mode at the moment.

They ran across large, tree-filled yards. They leapt little ponds and gardens with ease (that crazy quake ghost energy). They weren't maimed or anything, even though they were bleeding from my nose punch and they'd just leapt from a speeding truck onto pavement (again that energy). Paula was wild, though. Uncontrolled.

Please. What the hell's going on?

"Riley. They're coming. I can hear them. Flight!"

Riley listened with his ears, the same ones Paula was using to hear what? *Who? Who is coming?*

"The Shadows. They're coming! A big one! We have to get out of here," Paula cried.

Out of where? Riley thought.

"Everywhere! Flight! Flight!"

At the same time, Mouse and Mattheson were trying to chase Riley down. They weren't very far away, either.

"Did you hear that?" Mouse asked. "Somebody just crashed through the bushes back there."

"Uh huh," Mattheson said.

Mouse sprinted across a lawn and hurdled a short chain link fence. Mattheson almost jumped, but stopped instead.

"What's up?" Mouse shouted.

"My pants are too tight." It was true. Even in eighth grade, the dude wore seriously tight pants.

"How do you even skate in those? Come on!" Mouse cried.

Mattheson grabbed the top of the fence and hurdled it like a gymnast (straight-legged) then followed Mouse into the dark.

They set off a motion sensor and a large dog went crazy, ran at them barking until it reached the fence the two had just gone over.

They crouched behind a fat bush and tried to hold their breath. "This is stupid. Riley's just gone, bro," Mouse said.

Then, from the street, they heard a cry and then words, like one side of a conversation at top volume. "They're here! It's happening! Can we fight?"

"Oh shit, bro! That's Riley!" Mattheson shouted.

They sprinted to the neighboring street and burst from behind a parked car. There, a few houses away, they saw Riley standing frozen at the center of a cone of light. His eyes were super wide. His arms were held tense at his sides.

"Riley? Paula?" Mouse called. He slowly jogged up to him, while looking around nervously for what had caused Riley to cry out. Mattheson followed. "Are you okay? What's going on?"

Riley's arm bled badly. "They're here," Riley's mouth said.

"Who, dude?" Mattheson asked.

Just then, the streetlight above them began to buzz and snap. It went dim.

"Oh no," Mouse said.

"I . . . I can smell things," Mattheson said. "Bad things?"

"Oh shit baby Jesus," Mouse whispered as the air temperature dropped.

Their breath turned to steam. And then, down the street from them, a dark cylinder of Shadow rose slowly from a manhole (only visible because it was so much darker than the Encinitas night).

"That's one," Mouse whispered. "Rag-ass Shadow."

"Bitch," Mattheson said.

The boys and Paula were totally frozen in place. What grew in front of them was so strange, it was almost beautiful. From that small cylinder of darkness, rags, individual Shreds, began to unfurl and flap in the air, grow apart, then come back together into a whole, like the thing had exhaled, released, then inhaled. The figure grew human appendages, arms, a hooded head. The figure grew to twice the size of a normal man. It hovered just above the ground.

And then, the Shadow began to approach slowly. A wind sucked past the crew, towards the thing, as if it were sucking away oxygen. The dudes were buffeted and had to use all the strength in their legs not to get sucked away into it.

"Ahh," Mattheson growled. He bent over and clutched at his gut. "The air is hurting my stomach. It's . . . going through my stomach! I gotta . . . kill that thing!" Mattheson straightened and began walking like a damn maniac, stomping his feet hard into the pavement, so as not to get his ass vacuumed into the Shadow.

"Wait! Don't! What the hell, you dumbass?" Mouse shouted.

"Stop it, you bitch!" Mattheson cried at the Shadow. "Leave us alone or I will be forced to rip your stupid flappy body back to Shreds!"

The wind around them picked up, whistled in the scrub pine, sucked tumble weed and trash past them.

"Seriously, dude. Come on!" Mouse cried.

"You asked for it . . ." Mattheson called.

"Goddamn it!" Mouse shouted. He ran to the side of the road and searched the ground. Under a tree, he found pinecones, which he gathered up in his shirt.

"Flight! Flight! We have to run . . . we have to run!" Riley cried, but his body was stuck in place.

"Riley, Paula, whoever the shit you are, that thing wants to take a bite out of your ass. Get away!

"Riley won't move," Riley's face said.

"I'm gonna knock the shit out of it with some goddamn pinecones, but you go!" Mouse shouted. He turned and stomped toward the Shadow in the same way Mattheson did.

Riley's eyes stayed on the Shadow. "Flight. Please. Try," Paula said to Riley. His body moved, shuffled backwards, fighting against the wind. "I want to stay in your body forever," Paula said.

Then his body stopped. *I don't know. I don't know. We can't let those guys fight that thing for us,* Riley said from within.

"Then fight!" Paula cried.

But Riley couldn't move towards them either. He was frozen, terrified.

In front of them, Mouse caught up to Mattheson. They watched as Mattheson began jumping and punching, although still five feet away from the Shadow. Mouse exploded forward, screaming. He whipped pinecones.

The Shadow paused. Several pinecones sucked into the mass of flowing black rags. There was a series of crackles and pops, sparks, and then a flame rose inside the Shadow.

"Take that, bitch!" Mouse cried.

But the fire quickly disappeared and the thing wasn't harmed.

"Come on, bro! Let's go!" Mattheson shouted as he attacked like he would've back when he took a few weeks of tae kwon do in fifth grade (jumped up and down and punched and kicked up against the thing). But the first kick the dude landed became lodged in the Shadow's side. Mattheson hopped on his left leg. "Shit!" And tried to pull away. He turned back to Mouse, terror pasted across his face. "Bitch is cold! Froze my foot, man!" The Shadow seemed to look down at the hopping boy, then made a subtle gesture with its long arm, which launched dozens of speeding Shreds that enveloped Mattheson's body (he screamed), spun him into the air, then flipped Mattheson across the street, where he crashed face first into the middle of a pine tree. The Shreds spun, jammed him in deep. And up there in the tree, Mattheson stuck like glue. The Shreds swept away from the wriggling Mattheson, and flew back to the larger Shadow, like it was the mother ship. All except for one that is. One Shred swooped around Mattheson for a moment, then slowed, then hovered, then seemed to get an idea, like it wanted to become whole not with the Shadow but with our boy. It slid in close, heading towards Mattheson's lower back.

Mouse, who'd just witnessed all that craziness (which had taken place in the space of like five seconds), stood frozen in place. He still held a bunch of pinecones he'd planned on launching into the Shadow, but the attack on Mattheson had been like getting a hard slap on the head. He was stunned. But the little baby Shred heading towards Mattheson's back knocked the cobwebs out. "Oh shit, dude!" Mouse called. "There's something coming for you. There's this thing . . ."

Mouse dropped the rest of his cones, slipped on one, fell down, pushed himself back up, then sprinted towards Mattheson. "Dude, you gotta get down!" he cried.

"I can't!" Mattheson screamed. "I'm stuck, bro!"

Mouse leapt and grabbed Mattheson by the back of his pants, trying to rip him out of there. But those Shreds had jammed him in so deep, he couldn't be moved. Mouse's tugging had to have some effect, right? Mattheson's skinny jeans popped at the snap, opened wide, and slid down to Mattheson's knees, so that Mouse dangled from the dropped trousers and Mattheson's fruit-of-the-loom ass shone, exposed.

"This is how we're gonna die," Mouse cried.

Right then, the Shred pierced Mattheson's lower back, wiggled like a worm going down a wormhole. Mattheson screamed like a freaking banshee. And the Shadow turned its attention down the street to Riley.

The Shadow slid through the air toward them. It seemed to spread, grow. It picked up speed.

Mouse wrenched himself around to see what was happening. "Paula, run!" Mouse cried. He dropped from Mattheson's trousers and screamed, "Goddamn run, Riley!"

"Fight or flight," Paula said.

Okay, okay . . . flight, Riley thought.

And it was as if Riley's body was released from a trap. He exploded to the right, across the street, towards a wooded hill. Riley leapt up between the trees. He galloped through scrub, hurdling stumps and rocks, ducking under branches. "Go, go, go," he heard Paula say. His body sprinted as hard as it could, but a wind, a head wind, began to howl in his ears, battering him with leaves and branches, pulling him back, sucking air from his lungs. Something turned inside him then. He wanted to run further, faster. But Paula wanted him to stop.

Paula began talking fast. "It's too late. Too late. We have to fight now. Fight, Riley. We can fight. We can fight. We can beat this Shadow. We have to. You know how powerful we are together? We can do this. Riley!"

No, no, no, no, Riley said inside. *We have to get away . . .*

"We can't run from it. Fight it!" Paula screamed.

But the howling of wind, making his eyes dry, his mouth dry, his muscles dry, and the sound of his shoes crashing on rocky earth, heavier and heavier, and the wind blew so strong against Riley, and howled so loud in his ears, Riley couldn't make progress, and he couldn't make sense of anything, and a kind of heaviness, like rigor mortis, set into his arms and legs and lungs . . .

"Riley," Paula cried. "Please! We have to fight!"

Then, Riley later told us, neither he nor Paula could put together coherent thoughts. All he could do was feel the pain and the terror. Ice shot into his body's spine and grew up his back into the neck and head and brain, and cold wrapped his legs and squeezed, and he couldn't move and couldn't scream, and his muscles totally seized, froze solid like bricks, and Riley fell face first to the rocky ground.

The Shadow had caught him. It hovered over him. He remembers hearing the tattered fabric of the joined Shreds whipping above him. The thing reached down and rolled poor frozen Riley onto his back. Riley and Paula together stared in terror at the terrible eyeless being, this otherwise featureless face of darkness. Then, slow and sad, the Shadow extended its arm, pried open Riley's mouth with fabric fingers, reached into his throat with a dry as sandpaper hand and down. Riley's body shook so violently, choking, gagging, convulsing, and he could feel Paula's terror, but couldn't hear her anymore. Then he felt the worst thing he's ever felt, worse than how it felt to see his parents in handcuffs. He and Paula were ripped apart. The Shadow gripped her soul and tore her out from him. The pain in his gut seared and Riley couldn't breathe. *Paula,* he thought. *Fight . . .*

He lost consciousness. He fell through a black tunnel then out the other end. Riley breathed.

The darkness was terrible, impenetrable. The emptiness complete. Riley was in emptiness, part of emptiness. But then he felt pain. Was that pain? He hoped so, because he wanted to feel something, because feeling something meant that he probably wasn't dead out there in the dirt on some person's property . . . where what happened? Something . . . that thing . . . THE thing . . . the Shadow he'd seen in nightmares forever had become real and it did *what* to him? Riley breathed and his guts burned. He had never felt so alone in his life, which made no sense. He'd lost his parents and all his friends back in Utah and he'd been sent to live with his terrible grandparents who hated him, who hit him. But this was worse. This was way worse. This was a shittier loneliness, because someone so close to him, someone inside him? . . . Someone who was living inside him . . .

"Oh shit. What the hell?" Riley gasped for air. He forced himself to open his eyes. The trees hung down over him, but he could see light from the street, less than fifty feet from him. "Oh shit! Paula!" Riley cried.

He heard a voice echoing, not too far away. "Riley? Paula? Where the hell are you?" It was Mouse.

Riley rolled onto his side and pushed himself up to kneeling. He coughed and spit. Something wet and metallic had made its way into his throat. He spit again. "Blood," he said. "The Shadow ripped Paula out of me." He fell back over onto his face.

Out by the curb, Mouse cried, "Where in the shit are they?" He ran across the street and shouted into the bushes next to a giant house. "Riley! Paula! Come on!"

Mattheson had managed to wiggle out of the tree and pull up his skinny jeans. He didn't feel good, pals. Not at all. He took several steps behind Mouse then cringed, bent at the waist. "My guts, dude. I feel like . . . like bad gas, bro."

Mouse turned to him and nodded his head fast. "Yeah. I don't know. I think something went in you? In your back."

Mattheson spit on the ground. "Dude. I'm really bloated. Like . . . super bad." Suddenly a giant fart exploded from Mattheson. It rumbled deep but was also loud. It lasted like ten seconds.

"Holy baby Jesus," Mouse whispered. "You vibrated the earth, bro."

"There's more . . . there's so much more," Mattheson cried. "Something's totally up my ass, man. Totally."

"Okay," Mouse said. "Lay down, bro. Can you call Charlie or Wiz? See if you can get them out here to help us. I'll keep looking for Paula and Riley."

Mattheson bent further. Another fart let fly, this one longer and deeper, like the dying call of a moose or something.

"Oh no," Mattheson cried, as if all was lost.

They didn't even know they'd lost Paula.

CHAPTER TWENTY-FOUR

By the time Wiz's phone vibrated on the work table (it was plugged in, recharging), we'd been gathering stuff for a while. I'd dumped all the shit out of his giant backpack (into a wood box, so he wouldn't lose anything later) and had started packing different materials in there, shit he was slowly gathering from a supply closet (solar cells, wires, tools, a large battery, like big enough for a damn car, I swear). Instead of answering right away, we both just stared at his phone.

I looked at Wiz. "Aren't you going to pick up?" I asked.

"I don't know. I have a bad feeling," Wiz said

"No shit. Bad stuff is happening." I reached out and answered, "Who is this?"

"Ahhh!" Mattheson cried from the other end. "We can't find Riley and Paula! We got attacked by one of those rag bastards! And my farts are shaking street lights!"

"What? What about farts?" I asked.

"I got a Shred in my ass, bro! Oh Christ! My phone's got no battery. It's going dead. I'm possessed! We're on Los Morros, dude. Help!"

The connection ended.

"They're on Los Morros. Riley's still gone. Mattheson has really bad gas or something," I said. "Are we about ready, do you think?"

Wiz nodded. The guest book sat on the table. He reached for it. "Do you think we better bring this? Maybe Cortez will actually help us if he has it. Just in case I don't build the trap right?"

I nodded.

I lifted the backpack. He tucked the book under his arm. We made for the door. But then . . .

"Wizard? What in the hell you doing?"

We both spun around.

Gramps stood at the bottom of the stairs. He wore this grungy robe. "You heading out someplace this time of night?" Gramps asked.

"Uh . . . just back to the house. Going to bed," Wiz said.

"You're not stealing my materials and jacking my truck?" Gramps asked.

"Ha ha," Wiz said nervously. "No way!"

Gramps shook his head. "I don't care if you take the materials, but you and your little punk ass friends are not going to drive my goddamn truck. Put the keys on the work table before you go," Gramps said. He turned and headed up the stairs.

"Crap," Wiz said. He reached into his pocket and put the keys to the truck on the table.

A few seconds later, we were running down the path in the dark towards his house. Wiz sort of babbled while we ran. "No need to panic. It's fine. We'll get there. We'll figure out a way." It was pretty clear Wiz was trying not to panic. I know I was.

Without him illegally driving Gramps' truck, how could we possibly pick up Mouse and Mattheson, find Riley and Paula, then beat Cortez to Olivenhain Cemetery (where we figured we were most likely to find Rooster), build the trap and get all this shit over with? If we failed, what the hell would happen? Would we see Paula get ripped up? Would Rooster come after me? Was that possible? Would I literally die if we didn't kick Rooster's ass by dawn? At least I had my bike stuck in a bush by Wiz's house. I could move fast on that by myself. But could we carry the guest book, the trap materials, and ride double on my damn bike and do everything we needed to do? Wiz must've been thinking the same thing.

He stopped mid stride in front of me. I almost ran into him.

"I think I got a way for me to move faster," he said.

Although he hated to ride the stupid things, Wiz had a collection of kick scooters from when he was a kid. His dad thought he was into them. I guess Wiz rode one once at a toy store and his dad never saw him do anything remotely athletic, so he bought him six damn scooters over the course of a couple of years, trying to make Wiz normal.

"Hide by the truck, okay?" Wiz said.

I crouched down and watched Wiz make a beeline to the garage. He entered and a minute later came back out with a stupid kick scooter. I watched him go to the bush where Mouse and Mattheson's skateboards were stowed. He picked those up, dropped them, tripped on them, made a huge clattering sound, picked them back up and met me by the truck.

"We'll have to leave Riley's bike, but let's take the boards," Wiz said.

"We have so much shit to carry," I said.

"We'll never get this done if those guys have to walk, though," Wiz said.

"I'll grab my bike," I said.

"Good," Wiz said, but then he dropped the guest book and dropped the skateboards trying to pick up the guest book. "Shit!" he shouted.

And then a light turned on above. We both ducked fast. Wiz's dad stepped out onto the balcony surrounding the second floor.

"What in the hell is going on, young man?" Mr. Wisniewski called. From that high angle, he could see us trying to hide on the other side of the truck.

"Just . . . I have school work. My group!" Wiz said, standing up.

Mr. Wisniewski peered down at the pile of skateboards and the kick scooter and me holding Wiz's gigantically packed backpack. He shook his head. "I think you better come inside right now," he said.

"Uh, I can't. We're in the middle of an experiment."

"Now, or I call the cops on that kid next to you for trespassing."

"Goddamn it, Dad! I have to go!" Wiz shouted.

"Now!" Mr. Wisniewski shouted.

Wiz shook his head. "Oh no. This is bad," he whispered.

"Milton!" Mr. Wisniewski shouted. (Yeah, nobody calls Wiz Milton, but that's his real name.)

"Very bad," I whispered, nodding.

"You better go without me." Wiz dropped the kick scooters and the skateboards. He turned and stumbled into the house. He still carried the guest book, which I should've taken from him, because Cortez seemed like the only chance we had left.

CHAPTER TWENTY-FIVE

I rode my SE, Wiz's giant pack on my back filled with trap materials weighing me down from behind. I carried Mouse and Mattheson's skateboards in my left hand. Why even go to the damn trouble? Without Wiz, there was no way we'd figure out how to build a trap on our own. Cortez was our only hope, but Wiz had gone into his house carrying the guest book. Cortez wouldn't help us without it. I was so freaked out by the sight of Wiz's angry dad, I didn't even think to ask for it and I was too chicken-shit to knock on the door after Wiz was gone. And, worst of all, the street under me seemed like it was alive. I swear I could hear muffled howls coming from below. I swear the pavement vibrated. What Cortez said about the growing energy levels of Shadows, Shreds, ghosts, and what-the-hell-ever else was out there, seemed to be true. Scary as shit, pals.

I rode as fast as I could through darkness under dim, buzzing streetlights. At least Los Morros, where Mattheson called from, was close by. It only took maybe five minutes. I rounded a corner and saw what was left of my crew.

Mouse was kneeling over Riley (apparently he'd found him in some dude's yard and had dragged him out to the street underneath a street light). As I rolled up, I heard Mouse say, "They're here. We have to go, okay, bro? We have to get out of here."

I stopped the bike and dropped the boards on the street.

"This isn't over. We'll find her and save her," Mouse said.

"Who?" I asked.

"Paula, dude," Mouse said.

Mattheson lay on the side of the road some twenty feet away. He let the biggest damn fart I've ever heard (at least up to that point—I think I heard a couple of worse ones later). "Whoa. Shit." I almost laughed, even though I was pretty worried about what Mouse had just said. "What's going on with him?" I asked.

"Don't worry about the farts dude. Our girl is really, really gone. Rag ass thing ripped her right out of Riley's body."

I dropped my bike and stood over Riley. He had a little sticky blood under his nose. His mouth looked rubbed raw. "Are you okay?" Riley didn't answer. "Did the thing take her to Rooster?"

"We don't really know. Riley passed out while it happened," Mouse said.

Then Riley shook his head. He sat up slowly and in a voice that didn't sound anything like he had while Paula was in him, he said, "I'm not okay. I didn't fight."

"I don't think Riley and Mattheson should go to Olivenhain to meet Cortez," I said. "Can you take them some place?"

"My back yard, maybe," Mouse said. He thought for a second. "Yeah, that's good."

"Okay. I'll go meet with Cortez. I'll figure out how to build the trap. I'll stop Rooster." I looked down the road into the dark night. Truthfully, I was super scared. But there was only, like, three and a half hours left before all hell would break loose. What could I do? "Text me your address and I'll meet you there after."

Only then did shock pop up on Mouse's face. He looked around, then up the street. "Wait! Where's Wiz?" Mouse said.

"Dad busted him," I said. "He wouldn't let Wiz leave."

"Well, you're screwed then, dude!" Mouse spat. "Rooster's going to kill you and your death will haunt us for the rest of our lives."

"I have to stop Rooster!" I said.

Riley almost whispered. "Rooster has Paula. I know it. He won't be after Charlie anymore . . . You can go hide or something. "

Riley's words hung in the air. "Oh," I said. Riley might be right. If Rooster had Paula, wasn't I seriously off the hook? For like half a second I felt totally relieved. Then the weight of that shit fell on my shoulders. "Oh, so what?

I just let Rooster have her then? Let him shred her soul? Dudes, she came to us for help."

"Doesn't feel right," Mouse whispered.

"No," Mattheson moaned.

"No. I didn't fight. We have to help," Riley whispered.

But then the hopelessness of Paula's situation became real. I remembered what Wiz carried into the house with him. "Crap. I don't have the guest book. Cortez won't help me build the trap. There's no way to stop Rooster."

Sick old Mattheson groaned.

"We're all screwed. We're just stupid little kids," Mouse said. Then his face went pale. "Oh shit. Oh shit, what's that?" Mouse pointed up the hill.

A little light hovered and bounced in the darkness.

CHAPTER TWENTY-SIX

I thought Wiz was a rebel, because that's how I knew him. Since the beginning of the science project, he'd fought with me, called my dad crazy, shouted asshole at his own car (when he got dropped off at the coffee shop), allowed us to steal his gramps' pick-up truck, stole a bunch of trap materials from his gramps . . . the dude seemed willing to do anything, right? Apparently, though, Wiz was not a rebel at all before meeting us. He had never told his dad where to stick it. But then, that night after his dad busted us and made Wiz go inside instead of go fight the good fight with me and the crew, he actually did.

Mr. Wisniewski sat on the couch, sipping a gin and tonic, acting enraged that Wiz would leave the house in the middle of the night.

"You wanted me to have friends," Wiz said.

"I didn't mean miscreants. I saw that pack of trash you had over here."

That pissed our boy off. Why? Wiz (shock even to him) actually liked us! "Those guys are awesome. They're not trash."

Mr. Wisniewski shook his head and laughed. "Are they really awesome? As in epic? As in amazing?" (What a sarcastic dick.) "Go to your room, Milton. I've had enough of your bullshit for one lifetime."

Wiz stood. "Why don't you stick my bullshit in your butt."

"Ha," Mr. Wisniewski said. He lifted his drink to toast Wiz. "You'll love military school, kid."

Down in his bedroom, Wiz punched his Harry Potter pillows (before his obsession with steampunk, there was Harry Potter). "Asshole, asshole, asshole," he kept repeating. I guess he went after those pillows until he pretty much exhausted himself. Then he fell on his face on the soft rug. He turned his head to breathe and spotted the guest book on the floor nearby (he'd been so scared and then pissed off, he wasn't even aware that he'd carried it into the house with him).

"Oh no," Wiz said, sitting up. "Oh balls! Charlie's screwed." He knew trading that thing with Cortez was my only hope of getting a trap built.

He stood and kicked the book. It flipped over and fell on its spine. It opened to a large diagram filled with names and lines drawn across a tree. Wiz sank to his knees and squinted at it. He lifted the book to his face. *A family tree?* He hadn't seen this page when he'd looked at the book earlier. He ran his fingers over the tree. At the top, the oldest person on the tree, the head of the family: The Honorable John Hays, a judge. John Hays had a daughter and a son. The daughter married a man named William Kelly. Elinor Hays Kelly and William Kelly also had a son and a daughter. The daughter, Renata Kelly, married a man named Clarence Wilkins. Clarence *Wilkins* and William *Kelly* . . .

Wiz took in a fast breath. He ran his fingers down, across generations. Five generations down from John Hays, he located a girl named Paula Kelly. He ran his finger across the page. Six generations from John Hays, he located a kid named Charlie Wilkins (yeah, pals, me).

"Oh my God," Wiz whispered. "Paula and Charlie are related. That's why Rooster talked about fifth and sixth generations. They're cousins and Paula's the fifth generation after the old man John Hays. Charlie's the sixth!"

The door of Wiz's room creaked and closed.

"What?" Wiz gasped. "Is someone here?"

A breeze blew across Wiz's arms. The pages of the guest book turned right in front of his face. He sat back and shivered. The pages stopped turning on a yellowed newspaper article from 1922. The headline said: *Boy Strangled Dead at Olivenhain Cemetery.* Wiz read.

"Whoa. The hippie lied. Rooster wasn't killed in a car accident," Wiz said.

Wiz quickly read more.

Joseph "Rooster" Robinson, age 12.

Killed in fight with fisherman named Santiago Cortez, 36.

Cortez claimed the boy hid money and gold taken decades earlier from the Cortez family.

During his arraignment, Mr. Cortez shouted at the court. "I know the money's up there in Olivenhain. That Rooster boy got it hid. His family stole it from mine. I'll see him in hell."

Mr. Cortez pled guilty to murder in the second degree.

Wiz took a deep breath. "Okay. Okay. The hippie has to be Santiago Cortez's descendant. I bet the hippie is looking for the money," Wiz whispered. "But why did Charlie's dad have the book? And John Hays lived way too long ago to have anything to do with Rooster's murder. Why does Rooster want revenge on Charlie and Paula's family? They didn't kill him. The Cortez family did!"

Wiz leaned over the book, squinted, thought so hard, tried to make the connection between me, my dad, Paula, Cortez and Rooster. He didn't yet know anything about Yankee Jim Robinson and what that guy had to do with it all (although Yankee Jim was the beginning of it; he lived in the time of Judge John Hays). Wiz thought, "Come on, come on, come on . . ."

The ceiling light crackled above him. Wiz stared up at it. "Please help," Wiz said. The air felt warm. The breeze blew. The pages of the book turned. It opened to a map of Olivenhain Cemetery.

Wiz stared down. There were several Xs in different spots on the Olivenhain map. Possible locations, he wondered? X marks the spot, right? Maybe where the old stolen money and gold was stashed? Yeah, Probably! Cortez had said the quake would destroy his work. Would the tunnels under Olivenhain be destroyed? Would the treasure's hiding place be destroyed? Cortez really was running out of time if that were the case. Wiz shut his eyes and concentrated. This was simple math. *Rooster wants Paula or Charlie for some reason. Cortez wants the money. Cortez wants Charlie to meet him at Olivenhain with the book. The book contains Cortez's treasure map. He'd need that for sure, unless . . .*

Wiz's eyes snapped open. "Shit! He could deliver Charlie to Rooster in exchange for help locating the money!" Right then the door to his bedroom swung wide open. No one was there. A hot wind blew. "Okay. Okay. I've got to go," Wiz said.

And even though he figured he was writing his ticket to military school, Wiz grabbed a flashlight and a roll of duct tape from his desk drawer. He picked up the guest-book and placed it in an old backpack he rarely used anymore. He threw in his gramps' old night vision goggles. He swung the pack on his back. He tiptoed out into the hall and made his way through the dark to the garage. He pulled a kick scooter from the wall then expertly taped the flashlight on the handlebar. He opened the garage door as quietly as he could, and he was off, hoping he might still catch us over at Los Morros.

Lucky for us, Mattheson and Riley were both laid out from the Shadow attack. They had not been able to move fast or we might've missed Wiz.

Mouse had just said, "We're all screwed. We're just stupid little kids." And then he pointed up the hill. "Oh no, what's that?"

A little circle of light hovered in the darkness. Bounced. Got closer and closer.

"It's Wiz!" Mouse shouted. "Holy shit, it's Wiz!"

"Charlie!" Wiz shouted. "Cortez is a total liar!"

CHAPTER TWENTY-SEVEN

With Wiz back, we decided to stick together (there was no reason for me to go find Cortez by myself and Wiz convinced me pretty quickly that I should stay away from him if possible). We took off for Mouse's place, which happened to be very close to Olivenhain. It took us maybe twenty minutes to get there.

While it was pretty cool that we were all together (other than Paula, of course), things weren't that great. In fact, they were scary as shit. The sewers and streetlights on Los Morros moaned and buzzed.

I rode Riley on the back of my bike. Pedaled so hard, which was exhausting. He was a lump of damn flesh, man. He kept whispering, "I didn't fight."

I kept saying, "Shut up, dude. We have other stuff to worry about."

A dim streetlight shone down on the front of Mouse's place. The house was small. It was made of cracked stucco. A broken plywood skate ramp sat in the driveway. There was no grass in the yard. Just dried out old bushes and cactuses.

"You live in there?" Wiz asked as we pulled up.

"Yeah, my palace," Mouse said. "With Mom and my big ugly brothers, too."

Mattheson groaned. He stepped off his board and doubled over. Another cursed fart shook the earth around him. "I got to get to a lawn chair out back," he mumbled. "Need to stretch my guts . . ."

"Those farts are burning my eyes, bro," Mouse said.

They picked up their boards and entered. Wiz, Riley and I followed. In the house, two tall dudes, teenagers in stocking caps, snored on opposite ends of a long, broken couch.

"Your brothers?" Wiz whispered.

"Some of them," Mouse whispered back. "Go out back by the pool. We'll need power and energy for the rest of the night, so I'm going to make us some night tacos."

"Yeahhhhh," said one of Mouse's brothers, stretching and yawning. "Love sexy night tacos."

"I love tacos, too," Mattheson said, before folding over, moaning plaintively, and blowing a fart so loud it woke Mouse's mother in the other room.

"Dude. That was so amazing," Mouse's brother, Burt, said, sitting up straight on the couch. His eyes were huge. He pulled his hat off his head and covered his nose. "You're the king!"

An hour later, 3 a.m.— just one hour before Cortez was set to arrive at Olivenhain—Wiz leaned over a table in back of Mouse's house. It was bright as day out there, which I appreciated. Wiz had told me all that he knew about Judge Hays and how the old man was my great grandpa times six generations and that I was a distant cousin of Paula and how the puzzle about why it was her or me was beginning to make sense.

Mouse and his brothers had placed large floodlights around the yard (so they could skate all night in the empty pool). The light made Wiz's work on the trap easy enough. He screwed the frayed ends of a wire to the back of a one-by-one-foot black panel. I stood by Wiz's side, reading the schematic Wiz had drawn up in a notebook. The diagram was of a solar cell suspended on fishing string, connected to a battery capable of sucking in the energy of a ghost and holding it there, if only the ghost were to make contact with the solar cell.

Mouse sat on a white plastic deck chair across the table from us.

"So, wait a second. Say that thing about Paula and Charlie again?" Mouse said.

Wiz nodded. "Paula and Charlie are cousins. It's in the guest book. They're both related to a judge from the mid-nineteenth century," Wiz said. "Charlie's sixth generation. Paula Kelly's fifth. Rooster is after Charlie's family for some reason."

"Scary shit," Mouse said. "So, is there like a family curse?"

"Could you please let me concentrate?" Wiz asked.

Riley had been lying in a lawn chair twenty feet away. He hadn't said a word. He hadn't responded when Mouse's brother asked him how many tacos he wanted. I sort of thought he was going comatose and figured that was okay. What use was Riley without the ghost energy powering him? But suddenly he sat up. "Family curse?" he said. "Is that why your dad disappeared, Charlie?" he asked.

Silence fell across the crew. Mattheson, who lay by himself on the other side of the pool, made no noise. Wiz stopped turning screws. Everyone stared at me.

"He is gone, isn't he?" Wiz said. "He's not just on some mission."

I nodded slowly. I turned to Riley. "How did you know?"

"Paula knew," he said. "She told me."

"He's officially missing in action, but the government doesn't want us to tell," I said.

"That sucks, bro," Mouse whispered. "Why can't you tell?"

"Top secret, or something. But because we have to pretend he's okay, it's like we can't get over it, you know? That's what my mom says. I believe it, too."

Wiz sat forward. He put down the screwdriver. "Hey. Do you think what's going on now with us has something to do with your dad?"

I thought for a few seconds. "Yeah, but only sort of," I said. "I think my dad was into something bigger. I think my dad believed we're moving into a new age, into strange times. I don't think Rooster got him, though. But maybe something paranormal."

"Strange times, dude," Mouse said. "I'm sorry about your dad."

I could feel tears begin to rise up in my eyes. I couldn't let the sadness get me and drag me down the way it had been doing all year. I was so tired of being sad. Thank God Mattheson let a fart that sounded like a moose singing an old U2 song. It was like, *In the name of love . . .*

I began to laugh. Everybody else did, too.

"It's not funny," Mattheson moaned.

Riley stood up. He walked to the edge of the empty swimming pool. "Strange times," Riley said. "I can feel Paula. She's at Olivenhain Cemetery."

"That's where we're going," I said.

Just then Ben and Burt, two of Mouse's brothers, came out the back screen door carrying a tray of tacos. "Eat up, little men," Burt said. They put the taco tray down on some of Wiz's wires.

"Jesus!" Wiz shouted. "Careful!"

"Shut up, nerd!" Burt shouted. Then he laughed. "I'm just messing with you, bro." He stuffed a hot taco in his mouth.

Then both brothers grabbed skateboards from a wood box on the pool deck and dropped into the empty pool.

Riley, who later told me he had never turned down a taco in his entire life, couldn't eat. He didn't even want to smell the tacos. He stood and watched Ben and Burt skateboard back and forth, shooting up one wall, doing a sick little trick, then rolling back across. He thought, *she*

will be Shreds, nothingness, soulless, howling, unhappy Shreds.
Riley had begun to remember Paula's childhood, her dad
and mom, the stuff she hung on her bedroom wall. It was
like he'd lived her whole life. And her death. Paula had left
a residue inside him. He knew what Shreds really were.
He could picture the dark tunnels underneath the earth's
surface where she had roamed, homeless and afraid for so
long. He knew what it felt like not only to flee, to hide, but
to fight back, like Paula had the night she was murdered,
when Rooster, energized by a long ago earth quake, entered
her room from a tunnel, and attacked her, eventually taking her earth-bound life away with a cord, sharp, cutting,
that he wound around her neck.

Shit. Dude couldn't tell where Paula started and he
stopped. She was part of him, except she was gone. Part of
him was gone. Riley put his head in his hands. He longed
to have Paula back inside. There was actual joy in his body
when she was in there. *I love your body,* she'd actually said
to him.

"She loved my body," Riley whispered. He lifted his
head. "She loved my body. I have a body," he said. He
stood up. "I can fight. I can do stuff. I have a body." Mouse
looked at him from his deck chair, half a taco hanging from
his mouth. Riley said, "I love my body, too."

"Good for you, bro," Mouse said.

"I do. I've been shit. I love my body." Riley reached
down and grabbed Mouse's skateboard. He stood on the
edge of the pool, dropped the board and dropped in after it.

"Hey! You can't do that!" Mouse shouted.

No, Riley had never been a skater. Skating around earlier that epic day had been all Paula. But now, Paula was him, too, right? He crouched and shot across the pool and flew up the other side, launching himself high into the air. Riley gripped the board and waved at Mouse.

"Oh my baby Jesus," Mouse said.

"I'm a bird!" Riley cried as he landed.

"You're a magical tubby skate elf!" Mouse shouted. "So rad!"

Wiz and I both stood and stared at him. The sight was shocking, pals.

Riley shot up the wall on the other side. He grabbed the board and caught this gnarly rocket air, landing it easily.

"Is that real?" Mattheson asked from his chair. "Am I hallucinating?"

"It's real!" Mouse shouted.

Riley sped across the bottom of the pool, smiling huge. He winked at Mouse and pumped his fist and then he bailed pretty hard.

"You okay, bro?" Mouse asked, leaning over the edge.

"I'm really glad I'm here," Riley said, lying on his back. "I'm really glad I'm in my body and in a science group with you guys."

"I'm really pissed you're a better skater than me, bro," Mattheson said from his chair.

Riley stood up. "Is it time to go save Paula, yet?" he shouted.

"Just a few more minutes. Hey, how about you guys test the bug zapper on Mattheson's ass?" Wiz said. "Maybe we can burn the Shred, if that's what's up there causing the moose songs?"

I'll only say this: we did use the bug zapper on Mattheson and it worked. We cured his ghost ass (the Shred screamed inside Mattheson, which made his eyes bulge out and made him scream, which was scary, actually the only really scary part of the zap). There was some collateral damage, though, which was caused by a sick foot-long purple flame that came out of you know where. The ass portion of Mattheson's skinny jeans completely disintegrated and he had to roll around on the ground to stop all his clothes from going up in flame. Light from the Shred separated from the flame and it sort of happy danced off into the air. (Maybe Shreds can be released from their hell, right?)

We oohed and ahhed like we were watching fireworks. Then we slapped Mattheson with old beach towels that were on the dried out pool deck for some reason until the fire was out.

After that, we all ended up falling over and rolling around laughing, because the purple fire was such a damn shock and Mattheson screaming about his pants was pretty hilarious, also the whole thing was dangerous as shit. Holy balls, we laughed so hard.

Listen. I really love my crew. I thought that right then. So much better hanging with these weird dudes than my old friends and that douche sack Landon Anderson.

It was to be a night filled with burning pants, though. Things were about to get serious. At least we were a team.

CHAPTER TWENTY-EIGHT

At 3:30, Mattheson got back from his house next door, wearing the exact replica of the jeans that had just caught fire. A super restless Riley growled, "I can't wait any longer. It's almost four. We have to do something."

"Why are you tweaking, bro?" Mouse asked.

"Because. The Shadows are getting more powerful as we sit here. Rooster is getting more powerful. Morning is coming! You want Paula to be Shreds? You want a little part of her ending up giving some dude Mattheson Moose Ass?"

"I'm going as fast as I can," Wiz said. "But if Paula is going to have a chance, if Charlie's family is going to be safe, this has to be done right."

"Uh huh. Okay," Riley said. Then he dropped down on the pool deck and reeled off twenty push-ups.

Honestly, I sort of understood. We were supposed to meet Cortez at Olivenhain at four. If we didn't beat him there, what sort of surprise attack on Rooster could we have? Wiz even thought Cortez might want to trade me to Rooster for the treasure, right? I didn't really believe that. I didn't trust Cortez, but something told me he wasn't *that* evil. I didn't want to just walk right up to him, though. It seemed like we needed a good plan of attack. I stood up from my chair. "Maybe Riley and I should go over and check the Olivenhain Cottage in advance. We can figure out the lay of the land or whatever."

"No way," Wiz said.

"You really want to split up?" Mouse said.

"No, dude, but the time! We're running out of time!" I said. "Maybe we'll have better luck down there if we know what we are getting into before we show up with a bunch of ghost-catching equipment. Know what I mean?"

Wiz sighed. He nodded. "True. Okay. But stay the hell away from Cortez if you see him and don't get too close to the cottage. According to the Olivenhain overlay, there's a major ghost tunnel running right under it and one with portals in the middle of the cemetery. Stay to the right or far to the left, in the woods, and you'll probably be out of reach. I mean, I think. Take the bug zapper with you. But listen. Only use it if you know you're in trouble. I grabbed a better battery before we left the workshop, but I don't know how long the charge will last. Three or four zaps is all its got in it is my guess."

"Okay. Got it," I said.

We decided we'd meet at the end of the Olivenhain driveway in twenty-five minutes. Riley and I would do some investigating on site. Mouse and Mattheson would do some Internet research on the cottage while we were gone. Wiz would finish the trap as fast as possible. We'd meet and figure out next steps.

"Dope," Riley said. "Let's roll."

A few minutes later Riley and I made our way down the middle of the deserted Tres Hermanas Street. I rode my bike and carried Wiz's old pack with the bug zapper in it. I was getting better at hearing and feeling what was happening. Near manhole covers, the sounds of Shreds or Shadows from below grew. The street vibrated more there. "Steer clear of the manholes," I said to Riley.

He rolled right over the top of them (using Mouse's skateboard again) and laughed, because that was the kind of mood he was in (made me worry).

Dogs were being awakened by something, for sure. Every few minutes dogs barked and howled in houses and backyards for miles around. Maybe they were aware of what Cortez had said, that spirits and Shadows take energy from the shaking of the earth. But above ground where we rolled, I could see no signs of the paranormal.

It only took a few minutes for us to get to the edge of Olivenhain. And my heart dropped right away. No, I didn't see a ghost or ghoul or a giant, man-eating Shadow. There was a Jeep parked not more than a football field down the road from the entryway to the cemetery. I wished my phone was charged, so I could text back to

Wiz and the dudes (not that their phones had any charge left by that point either).

"Do you recognize that car?" I asked Riley.

"No. Should I?" Riley said.

"It's Cortez. He must be in there already."

"So?" Riley shrugged.

"So, maybe he's setting a trap for me?" I didn't want to believe it, but that's what Wiz would think, right?

"We'll be careful," Riley said.

Instead of taking the skateboard and the bike with us, we hid our wheels behind a stand of short palm trees and then snuck through the brush. As we walked up the drive, I remembered what Wiz said. I pulled Riley off the road and tried to stay left of the cottage, away from the cemetery and its tunnels. The going was tough. It was pretty much pitch black, except for the light of the half moon (not much!). There was no path ahead of us and the grasses were tall. We eventually walked into groves of scattered trees. The mowed cemetery spread to our right. Beginning where we were was unmown, and we had to shuffle and push brush and sharp grass aside. Suddenly my foot caught on something rock hard. I fell forward onto my chest.

"Ouch. What the hell?" I asked.

Riley stomped over tall, dry grass and revealed a weathered gravestone barely lit by the moon above. "'Martha Fitzpatrick, 1872-1873.' Looks like you tripped on a dead baby's grave," Riley said.

"Here? We're in the trees. We shouldn't be in the cemetery at all."

"Proof is in the pudding," Riley said, kicking the gravestone. He turned and pushed aside grass around us, which revealed more old stones.

"I don't know, man. I guess there could be a ghost tunnel beneath us then. I thought we were away from the cemetery."

Immediately after I said that, I felt a vibration below me, the earth shuddered. Something groaned nearby.

"I think we're getting close," Riley whispered.

"Yeah, but to what?" I asked.

"Ghosts," Riley whispered. "Girl ghosts." His eyes were huge, glowing in the moonlight.

"Let's keep going," I said. "I don't think Wiz was right about the layout of the cemetery, though." I pushed myself up to standing and began walking, more carefully. I didn't pay attention to Riley. I didn't think I had to. I figured he'd stay right behind me.

I moved on into the darkness in front of us.

CHAPTER TWENTY-NINE

Meanwhile, back at Mouse's place, he and the no longer super farty Mattheson researched on the Internet and paged through the guest book. From the historic pictures online, the Olivenhain Cottage didn't seem like much. It was squat, one-story, sat on a little rise overlooking the old cemetery. It had served as the home for generations of care-takers, gravediggers. Mouse stared at images on his mom's laptop. "Weird, bro. Just looks like a piece of shit old house I wouldn't want to go into."

"We definitely don't want to go into it," Wiz said, turning screws, connecting wires to the photovoltaic cell. "We're going to have to, though, probably."

"Yeah, well we're probably going to all die like chumps. I just read a description in the guest book that says the Olivenhain floors are filled with trap doors and one of its rooms drops about a hundred feet into the damn ground. That's the perfect spot to capture and destroy the dope little body of a dude like me," Mouse said.

Wiz took a deep breath and looked at the assembled ghost trap. On one hand, it made sense to him. The ghost's essence, or whatever, is carried in light energy and, like sunlight, when the ghost hits the photovoltaic cell, the semiconductors inside will convert the ghost's light protons into electrical current, which will travel the wires and get stored in the battery. Then what? "Are we going to throw the battery in a dumpster after Rooster is in it?" Wiz asked.

"Yeah, an Arby's dumpster. That's the right place to throw a ghost battery," Mouse said.

Wiz nodded. "Arby's," he said. "Screw Arby's."

"Why? Arby's is pretty good," Mattheson said.

Wiz looked up from the trap. "Almost done. We're just about ready to go. Hope Charlie and Riley are getting some good information."

CHAPTER THIRTY

I was getting close to good information, maybe. But the ground around me felt alive, like it was breathing, like the grass was snaking. That made my heart smack hard in my chest. There was no sign of Cortez, which made me think he must be inside (he just said to meet him at the cottage, not inside it, though). I neared the left-most flank of the cottage and thought about how Dad might approach surveillance. He would never get in full view of a window. He'd do his best to stay out of sight lines on the outside of the house, too. Lay low. Move from obstruction to obstruction. There was a stand of sharp-tined bushes to the left of the building, some twenty yards from the front door.

"Let's get up by those and lie down, see if we can hear anything," I whispered to Riley. "Maybe Cortez isn't in there, but if we end up going in later, it would be cool to know if he is."

Riley didn't respond. I looked behind me. Nobody.

"Aw shit, what the hell?" I whispered. I waited for a moment for Riley to follow me from the trees. Still, nobody. "Damn it, Riley." I figured I better do the reconnaissance on my own. Wiz and the crew would be at the end of the drive waiting for us soon. I thought, *Please Riley, don't be abducted...* Then I ducked and ran to the bushes and lay down in the tall grass underneath the tined branches (I really felt like the grass was alive, though!). I stayed there for a couple of minutes, staring into darkness. The ground shook slightly. There was a quiet chorus of moans, like dozens of people softly saying *ah* all at once. The hair stood high on my damn neck.

And then I saw it. Riley emerged from the trees forty feet to my right. He walked stiffly toward the front of the house.

"What the shit? Hey. Riley. Shit. Stop!" I called.

But he didn't stop! He was like a zombie. He teetered towards the house. And then, about ten steps from the edge of the trees, on what I guess you'd call the cottage's lawn, it was like the earth completely lost its solidity around Riley. He stopped in place and looked down. I shouted. He turned and looked at me, totally confused. The ground puckered like lips. It popped. A hole opened. Warm, steam hissed upwards like a cancerous breath!

"Uh oh," Riley said, looking at me.

The hole puckered again and sucked him into the earth.

"Holy shit!" I cried. I scrambled out from under the bush then ran to where Riley had just been swallowed. I got there in time to take a giant, disgusting sulfur gust of gas in the face. The hole slowly closed before my eyes. Without thinking, I just dropped onto my stomach and reached into the hole, reached for Riley. The earth wrapped around my shoulder and crushed it. I screamed.

And then a small burst of light appeared in front of me. I strained to pull my head off the grass, to stare at the thing. The light spread. Arms grew out from its sides, legs dropped from it, but didn't reach all the way to the ground. The light shivered. "You will be cold," said a child's voice. "So cold, Charlie Wilkins."

"Get away from me Rooster!" I shouted. With the arm that wasn't stuck in the hole, I tried to pull the bug zapper out of the pack on my back. I still can't believe I hadn't taken it out before just because I was afraid if I fell down again I might break it. But I had to use it, so it had to be out, but it wasn't!

"You're at my house," Rooster said. "I can do what I want here."

Rooster suddenly condensed into a pinprick of light. For a moment I stopped struggling, because I thought maybe he was going away. But then the little prick began to glow bright and then brighter. It spread out into a buzzing cord of light, which slowly closed in on me.

"What are you doing?" I whispered.

I got my answer immediately. The cord fired from a few feet away and wound around my neck. I remember struggling, trying to pull at it, twisting back and forth, kicking the ground, but I couldn't win and I couldn't breathe. My head began to feel like it was going to explode. My eyes watered. My eyes burned so bad. My eyes closed.

And, yeah, I did feel so cold. At least for a moment.

CHAPTER THIRTY-ONE

"I'm done. This thing is operational!" Wiz shouted. The ghost trap sat on the surface of the table next to him, photovoltaic cells hung from fish wire on a bolted metal frame. The cells were connected to an electric lawn mower battery by several feet of wires.

Mouse and Mattheson clapped.

"Hell yeah, bro!" Mouse said.

Wiz looked at his watch and knew they were in deep shit, though. "We're suppose to meet Charlie and Riley in like four minutes."

Mouse and Wiz stared at each other across the table next to the swimming pool. "We won't make it by four o'clock. What if Cortez gets there before us? Charlie doesn't even have the book!"

"Hippie might go ape shit!" Mattheson said.

"I'll see if Barton can give us a ride over there," Mouse said. He kicked back his chair and ran into the house.

Luckily Barton's so chill.

Just like a minute later, Wiz, with the help of Mouse and Mattheson, placed the photovoltaic ghost trap in the open hatchback of Barton's car. Wiz stepped back and surveyed the scene, took a quick look at the bubble-shaped orange car. Wiz knows his cars. He knew it had to be built in the 1970s.

"Is this a Ford Pinto?" Wiz asked.

Barton, who had long straight hair that went all the way down to his ass, nodded, "Yeah, bro. Sickest shit ever built in America."

"Don't Pinto's blow up if they get hit from behind?" Wiz asked. "I read about them in a book about the worst cars ever made."

"True. Guess the gas tank is right where it shouldn't be! Dope, huh?" Barton said.

"Dope?" Wiz said.

"Dude, we don't got time for your fear," Mouse said. "Get in!"

A few seconds later they cruised towards Olivenhain. "Speed up, Bart. We have shit to do," Mouse said.

"I got a warrant for parking tickets. Can't attract cops, dude."

"This is serious," Mouse said.

"All right." Barton hit the accelerator and the Pinto fishtailed down the road.

CHAPTER THIRTY-TWO

In a way, the crew was already too late, though, because, right about then, I lost consciousness from Rooster strangling me.

But I didn't just black out. It was more like my eyes closed and I fell, tumbled through a trap door, away from Olivenhain, down into something else completely. I woke from blackness to the sound of hot air screaming in my ears. I fell through dark banks of clouds or smoke (smelled sour). I couldn't tell if it was real or if I was dreaming. Then my back smacked against rock (it didn't hurt), but not a floor, more like the side of a chute, which I slid down, crashing over bumps, bouncing into deeper dark, accelerating down, down, down. I tried to scream but I had no voice. And it was like I was going a hundred miles per hour, maybe two hundred, through dark and then a hot dimness, an orange heat blasting my face. I rounded some kind of curve and then the chute I rode shot straight down, like the end of some big beast's insides and boom, I got fired out the ass.

I crashed to a stone floor, where clearly I should've died, but I didn't. It was like my ribcage crushed, broke, totally collapsed then reformed, and I sucked for air like a dude who almost drowned . . . "This is a dream. This is a dream. This is a dream," I told myself.

The floor was so hot. Small rocks, like gravel, fell from the ceiling, hit me and burned. Fires blew up and then sucked away. I kneeled. Looked for a way the hell out of there. "Crazy dream!" I shouted. "Wake up!"

"No!" croaked a voice. "This ain't no dream!"

There was an explosion behind me. I spun, still kneeling.

"Why you here, Charlie?" The voice sounded like it came from a giant bullfrog.

I pushed myself up. "Who said that? Who's talking?"

"Or are you spongy? Did a ghoulie take you, too? Aw, damn, if Rooster got your body, we're out of it. We're done. Nothing left but lost treasures and shredded souls."

The voice echoed around me. I spun again. And there, through rolling smoke, a large figure walked. I totally froze. Whatever was coming towards me was huge! Big gut, big beard, big hair . . . *holy shit!* Cortez, except I could see through him. I could see the fires burning behind him! It was like he was made out of thin paper.

I crouched to take off. But Cortez shouted. "Don't run, buddy. You're still solid! There's hope! I can get you out of here and you can still get this thing done!"

"I'm solid? What are you?"

"I'm just energy. Yankee Jim has my body!"

"Who is Yankee Jim?" I shouted.

"The dead bastard responsible for all our hell!"

A large black bird dove from the roiling smoke above. It clawed at Cortez's see-through hair.

"Damn it! No more time to explain. That bird will take your eyes out!"

The bird circled back and went at Cortez's head again.

"Bitch!" Cortez shouted, swinging his see-through fist. The bird swooped back up, its feathers whistling in the hot air. "Birdies want you to stay down here with them. But we got to get you out, or we're both goners!"

Cortez took off walking, long, mighty steps. I stayed locked in place.

He turned back. "Follow me, little dude! And try not to remember what you're going to see. It's not going to make sense, anyways." Cortez took off.

The walls trembled. The ceiling began to cave. Giant stones the size of cars and trucks began to fall.

I spun around trying to locate . . . I couldn't remember who I'd been with. I could sort of picture Cortez, but I couldn't remember who he was. I couldn't remember what I was doing there. I began to totally lose my shit. I screamed. I don't even know exactly what words fell out of my mouth, but I know it was sheer terror, and the more I screamed, the more the room around me glowed, until fires began to burst from the walls. Smoke filled the space and my eyes and my lungs. I choked and gasped and fell to the floor where I was ready to just be done.

But a large hand grabbed me under my armpit, lifted me up, slid my body over this big shoulder, took off running with me, as if I was a tiny kid.

This is so weird. But I could smell him. I knew him.

"Dad?"

"Charlie."

"Are you here?"

"Yes. Shut your eyes."

He ran. I didn't shut my eyes. It was like fear itself chased us. And fear grew in the form of a huge, hissing Shadow, the black fabric flaring into the air, filling all space, blocking out all light and hope. It came after us without seeming to move at all, the tethers of fabric rapidly extending towards us.

"It's coming, Dad. The Shreds!" I cried.

"Nothing is real. Everything is real, Charlie. I said shut your eyes."

We fired into a tunnel that tightened with every footstep. The walls burned, the tunnel squeezed us. Dad fell to his knees. Crawled. Cupped my little kid body against his beating chest. Tethers of fabric tore at Dad's feet, wrapped around his knees, but Dad kept kicking forward, moving forward. A bright light shone at the end of the tunnel ahead. Dad strained and pushed. The Shadow's force, its gravity was huge. This howling wind. Dad cried out, pushed his shoulders through the opening into . . .

The bright sky. Orange sky. Rock beach. Mighty ocean in front of me. Cortez held my hand. His big beard was covered in soot. His eyes burned red under his heavy eyebrows.

His mouth quivered. The hippie broke down. "Charlie, my boy," Cortez said. Tears began to run down his cheeks into his beard. "You listen to me right now, kid. No one is ever gone. Do you understand? Everything changes. All matter changes. Energy cannot be destroyed. No one is ever gone from you."

I nodded. I could barely take this all in.

"My baby boy. I love you so much. I'm sorry . . . Now swim. You just swim hard." It was Cortez saying all this.

Then Cortez picked me up over his head. He said, "When you fight my body in that house, remember it's not really me. It's the murderer Yankee Jim Robinson. Go for the damn balls!" And then, Cortez threw me into the ocean.

Light, sky, splash. I bobbed on waves.

Cortez cried from the rocky shore, "Swim, Charlie! Go!" He was engulfed in shadow. Then reaches of shred fabric stretched out across the surface of the ocean for me. Those tethers that touched water immediately turned to steam, hissed and dissolved. I sucked for air, shut my eyes, then dropped, dove, and swam deep down into the water.

My arm released from the hole. The hole in front of the Olivenhain Cottage that Riley had disappeared in. It felt like I'd been gone for hours. All was dark. All was silent. I fell back onto my ass.

Then the ghost boy Rooster manifested fully formed in front of me, a boy made of light.

I lost my breath. "Please leave me alone," I said.

He began to fade. "Your father saves you," he said quietly. "My Uncle Yankee sends me to hell."

And then with a static snap, he was gone.

"What just happened?" I whispered. There was dead silence. No wind. Absolute stillness.

Until Riley's scream.

CHAPTER THIRTY-THREE

The Pinto pulled onto the Olivenhain Cemetery drive-way. I wasn't there, but I know the dudes were tweaked. Wiz's breathing became more and more shallow. "I could just go to military school," he whispered. "But here I am, fighting with ghosts . . ."

That was the first mention Wiz made of the potential doom in his future. "Military school?" Mattheson asked.

"What?" Mouse asked.

"Never mind," Wiz said.

Barton braked, stopping the Pinto just past the intersec-tion of the street and the cemetery drive. There was no light on, anywhere. Only the moon above made it possible to see at all. "Why's it so damn dark, you donkeys?" Barton asked.

"This whole area is a dark sky zone. They don't allow street-lights in here by law," Wiz said. "Preventing light pollution."

"Dumb!" Barton said. "Why are we here?"

"We're going to trap a ghost, bro. Keep it from shredding Charlie and this other ghost chick," Mouse said.

"Rad," Barton said. "I'll stay in the car."

Mouse leapt out. Wiz and Mattheson followed. Wiz pulled the Stock Shock cattle prod out of the Pinto's trunk and handed it to Mouse. "Fire this while touching a Shadow or Shred or whatever and it should suck out the thing's energy."

"Look out, ghoulies," Mouse said.

Then Wiz and Mattheson lifted the ghost trap out.

"So, where the hell are they?" Mouse asked. He looked around. Of course, Riley and I were otherwise engaged. By then, Riley had been sucked into the damn ground and I had been strangled and fallen into some kind of burning hell!

"Who?" Mattheson asked.

"We're pretty late. I wonder if they ran into Cortez or something?" Wiz said.

"They're not here, that's for sure," Mouse said.

Wiz nodded. They all took deep breaths. "You guys ready for this, then?" Wiz asked.

"For what?" Mattheson asked.

"Hell yeah," Mouse said. "Let's go up there and see what ass we can find to kick."

"Up where?" Mattheson asked.

Wiz pulled on the night vision goggles Gramps used in Vietnam (not exactly high tech, but functional), then turned and began the walk up the drive. Mouse carried the Stock Shock. Mattheson carried the trap.

"Seriously. What are we doing?" Mattheson asked.

The Pinto's headlights lit the path in front of them for about a hundred yards, then fizzled out, leaving the rest of the road in darkness. Just as they made their way to the edge of the Pinto's light, an odd scream pierced the night air.

"Holy shit. I don't like the sound of that, bro," Mouse said.

"Was that Riley?" Mattheson asked.

"Whoever. It was bad," Wiz said. "Let's go."

The three ran up the drive, over the throbbing tunnels. Wiz completely forgot the advice he'd given to me, to stay far left or far right when approaching the cottage.

For my part, I was up the cottage steps in a heartbeat. I'm not dumb. I definitely wanted to be prepared before encountering Shadows or whatever this time (I didn't want to get strangled again and sent to . . . I couldn't even begin to understand what I'd just been through . . . had Cortez saved my life? or had my dad?). Before I threw open the door, I stopped, exhaled, pulled the pack off my back, and pulled out the bug zapper. Then, with my right hand, I pulled on the door. As soon as I did, something so weird happened. The door turned to thick liquid for a split second, fused into the doorframe, and re-solidified. So scary.

"Help! I'm stuck in the floor!" Riley screamed from inside.

"Aw, piss!" I reared back and kicked the door. It didn't budge. "I'm looking for a way in," I shouted at Riley.

He didn't respond.

I didn't know what to do next, so I can't even tell you how excited I was to hear three sets of feet running up the drive behind me.

"Charlie!" Mouse shouted. "Where the shit have you been!"

"Shh," Wiz said.

"Riley's locked inside. I got sucked to hell. Shit's crazy, man!" I shouted.

"Sucked?" Mattheson asked.

"Calm down," Wiz said. He climbed the steps onto the porch and pulled on the door. "That's solidly fused."

Mattheson put the ghost trap down on a step. "I'm a master door breaker. Mom forgets her keys all the time, so . . ." Then he climbed the steps, leaned back and kicked the door hard (I'll grant him this, a shit load harder than I kicked it). It didn't budge. He ran back into the lawn, ran up the stairs, leaped and kicked, which shot him backwards back down the stairs. "Like kicking a rock!" he cried.

Wiz looked around the yard with his night vision glasses. "Maybe there's another way in?" He stepped off the porch, moved to the right, looking up at the cottage's roofline.

I followed him. Mouse backed up (I think to get a wider view, even though it was so dark I doubt he could see anything). Mattheson ran and kicked the door again. This time he flew back and fell onto the drive.

"Stop, Mattheson. You're shaking the ground. You want to wake up all the dead people in this cemetery?" Wiz hissed.

"Why is the ground still shaking?" Mouse asked.

I could feel it, too.

"Oh . . . You guys feel that?" Mattheson cried.

"Ahhhh!" Riley cried from within.

We all turned back towards the cottage. I gasped. Small strands of shadow shot from the chimney like bats. They glowed in the light of the moon. They danced back and forth across the front of the house and increased in number second to second.

"Holy balls," Wiz said. "Holy shit!" he shouted. "The Shreds are gathering!"

They wove themselves into a torrent then spun around us like a tornado on TV. Mouse pulled the Stock Shock out of his pants and began zapping them like crazy, small cracks of green light and smoke that smelled like death. Mattheson rolled over to him. Mouse did his best to protect them both.

Wiz hunkered down next to me and cried, "Bug zap! Bug zap!"

"Got it." I still held the zapper in my left hand. I pressed the button on the bottom. A buzz emitted from the thing for a moment and then a crack like lightning pierced the air. For a split second every one of the thousand Shreds within ten feet of us froze in place. They glowed green then turned to smoke and ash. "Yes!" I cried.

Unfortunately, the Stock Shock could only get one at a time. I crawled toward Mouse and Mattheson with the zapper. When I was within about ten feet, I pressed the button again and braced myself for another crack of lightning. But nothing happened. Maybe the battery needed time to recover? I didn't know.

I looked up in time to see Shreds lift Mouse and Mattheson from the ground. Shocks of green light emitted from the cloud that carried them. Mouse was still doing his best to fight, but, really, he was way over-matched. The cloud rose up over the cottage and then shot back down the chimney. Mouse and Mattheson were gone.

I screamed. "They're in the cottage!" I turned back to Wiz. But he wasn't there! I mean, he was nowhere. Just gone! "Wiz?" I cried. He didn't answer. Shreds began to close in on me. I pressed the zapper button again and again. Nothing. I fell on my side and covered my face. I curled into a ball.

But then a loud, thumping music rose into the air. The source was some place down the drive, down toward the street. The Shreds that had collapsed around me seemed to stall their advance. They moved off me, paused, almost like they were listening to the music.

It was old school punk.

The Shreds rose and bounced to the sound of the beat. I slowly sat up. I watched this all take place . . .

A few minutes earlier, back at the Pinto, Mouse's brother Barton had slid a Black Flag cassette into the tape deck. Dude loves Black Flag. Right as he did so, he spotted a set of headlights in his rear view mirror. The car slowed. Seemed to check Barton out. *Cop car!* A second later, the car rolled on, but the cop spooked Barton, for sure. He turned the ignition and slowly drove up Olivenhain Drive. *Got to get out of sight of the piggies . . .* That's what he told me later. When he stopped and turned off his headlights, the darkness sent shivers up his back and down his legs. He turned up the volume on the Pinto's stereo. *My war!* Henry Rollins' shouted. Black Flag always gave Barton courage. "Why don't you try it, dark sky!" he shouted out the window. "Just try to mess with me. My war!"

He didn't know that Shreds, by their very nature, love Black Flag, too.

Barton banged his head repeatedly into the steering wheel. As he did, a thousand Shreds, the remains of ripped souls, swarmed the Pinto.

Barton's eyes were shut tight. He banged the wheel again and again and again. And then, when Henry shouted "*Yeah! Yeah! Yeah!*" Barton banged his face on the wheel so hard his nose began to bleed. "Ow, bitch!" he cried. He reached down and grabbed a wad of his t-shirt and pressed it to his face. Tears rose up in his eyes.

Then he heard some, like, flapping? Really, like a flag flapping in the wind? Like maybe a lot of flags flapping? Flags flapping louder than his sick stereo could blast Black Flag itself?

Barton opened his eyes and let tears slide down his cheeks. He couldn't see, so he blinked. The flag flapping sound was so damn loud! He pressed his bloody shirt into his eyes hard, blinked more. Something, right on the other side of his windshield seemed to be moving, squirming, like, weaving.

"What the hell?" Barton cried.

He shut his eyes hard. He muttered, "This is not real, bro. Just hallucinating from concussing your face, right?" He opened his eyes again. Thin arms of black fabric reached in through the open window. "Ahhhhhh!" Barton screamed.

He scrambled, turned the key, floored the gas, popped the clutch, and shot off up the hill towards the cottage, gravel firing everywhere, Shreds sliding in through the windows, attaching to his face and neck.

I couldn't believe what I was seeing. Shreds from all over (from the chimney, from the ground in the cemetery, from the trees) lifted into the air and fired in a swirling mass, towards this car, the damn Pinto, which fishtailed up the hill toward me, while also blaring that crazy punk music. Shreds covered it completely. I could hear Barton screaming inside it. The Pinto spun around a bend near the cottage, shot pellets of rock and chunks of cemetery turf into the air. It slid, spinning wheels, heading right at me. "Uh oh." I ran and leapt up onto a porch step, right next to the ghost trap (where Mattheson had put it before trying to break down the door). The car spun 180 degrees in front of me, shooting gravel and dirt into my face, then fired straight into a tall pine tree. The windshield popped out and shattered against the tree. Shreds dove into the car, a giant flow throbbing to the sound of Black Flag. Barton screamed and screamed and apparently threw the car in reverse. It roared backwards, spun out. Then it headed directly for me and the front of the cottage going backwards at huge speed.

"Oh shit!" I shouted. I bent down, picked up the two heavy pieces of the trap (solar cell and car battery) and jumped out of the way just as the car's back end came in contact with the front side of the cottage. I rolled behind a bush.

And, a Pinto's gas tank is right where it shouldn't be.

The explosion was amazing. Powerful. Fiery.

Lucky for Barton, the windshield had already popped the shit out, because the force shot Barton out of the front of the Pinto like a damn cannonball. He flew about a hundred feet back down the road and landed on his chest. I watched from the bush as Barton pushed himself up and ran naked from the waist down into the cemetery. His pants had apparently burned off.

The Shreds weren't so lucky. We definitely know now that they're flammable (Mouse had used a zippo lighter to burn them before, but somehow we didn't think of that—should have had a flame thrower with us). Anyway, the gasoline fire spread across the mass of ghost fabric, incinerating and releasing the energy within.

So weird.

The destruction was shiny, sort of sparkly, like full of happiness. The light that rose off the burning Shreds into the near-dawn sky hummed, like sang. It sounded like a chorus of happy chipmunks rising into the dark. Shreds don't want to be Shreds. They love to be released.

"Whoa," I whispered.

An orange glow intensified behind me. I turned and looked at the cottage. Barton had blown a big hole in it. Fire began to spread. My first thought was that I should run like hell to get away. I'd already been through so damn much that night, plus police and fire trucks were going to show up at some point, but then I heard Mouse, Mattheson, and Wiz shouting from inside. I had to get to them out.

CHAPTER THIRTY-FOUR

Like a dumbass, I dropped the ghost trap and climbed into the hole in the cottage. I immediately located the dudes. They were all jammed sideways in the cottage's fireplace. The fire must've incinerated the Shreds that carried them in. They were covered in ash, but seemed okay (except for the fact they were jammed into the chimney of a burning house!).

The room was small and windowless. The fire sucked air from outside, making it windy as shit. Wiz was on top of the other two. His entire waist was outside the fireplace.

"Just pull my arm!" he shouted.

I reached down and pulled as hard as I could. They were so damn stuck. We both screamed with the effort of it.

"Maybe if we bounce, bro?" Mattheson shouted.

"Yeah! We'll bounce your ass up and down while Charlie yanks you!" Mouse cried.

"That sounds so dirty," Wiz said.

But it worked. While I pulled on Mouse's arm, the two of them shook underneath him. Wiz slid out.

"I think I heard Riley shouting in the next room," Wiz cried. "Go get him and I'll get these guys out."

I didn't even think. I bolted across the room and pulled open the door. "Riley?" I shouted.

"Yeah?"

And there he was, stuck in the floor up to his chest, like he'd fallen into a hole. "I'm here, dude!" I shouted. I stepped into the room and the door slammed shut behind me. "Shit!" I turned and tried to open it, but no way, the thing was sealed like the cottage's front door had been before Barton's Pinto blew it wide. Without the door open letting in the light of Barton's fire, there was total darkness.

A voice called in the dark, "Wilkins child, we let you go once, but if you insist on entering, I'm going to have to insist you die."

I dropped down to the wood floor. That voice wasn't Rooster. That wasn't a kid. That was a scary-ass man.

"Paula's below me," Riley whispered. "She's in a hole right below me."

I crawled toward his voice. "Keep speaking, man," I said.

"Cortez and Shadows have her. They're just waiting for the quake so they can shred her, man. Get me out of this hole!"

The floor I crossed was so sticky, like covered in drying blood. The smell was horrible, too.

As I reached Riley, Wiz began pounding on the door. "It's locked tight. Charlie!" he shouted.

"I know! Can Mattheson break it?" I shouted back.

"It's burning down out here!" Wiz shouted.

But Mattheson, who must've gotten out of the fireplace, didn't care, because he immediately started kicking at the door. It didn't break open.

Even though I couldn't really see Riley, I could locate his left arm, the one that wasn't jammed in the hole. I grabbed onto it and pulled. He didn't even remotely budge. I wasn't tall enough to pull him up, plus Riley already weighed like 200 pounds. Pulling him to the side wouldn't do any good. Still, I tried. Riley cried out in pain (think jagged wood floor boards crushing into your ribs).

The voice from before laughed. Then it said, "The only way out is down, Wilkins child."

I pulled as hard as I could and Riley screamed. Mattheson pounded on the door.

"We're going to have to get out!" Wiz screamed from the other room.

Fine, I thought. *Down it is.* I put my hands on Riley's big head, located his shoulders.

"What are you doing?" he said.

"Shut up," I said. Then I jumped straight up in the air and landed on him. The floor around us gave way and we crashed down into a deep cellar below the cottage. We hit hard, dirt floor. The darkness was intense. I groaned.

Riley shouted, "Paula! We're here! We're coming for you! Get ready!"

"Ready?" said a deep voice behind me. I twisted around. The flame of a torch suddenly illuminated the entire space. A smiling, red-faced Cortez held it aloft. Large Shadow creatures stayed back from the flame, hovered in the corners. "My Rooster couldn't kill you, could he?" Cortez said. But it didn't sound like Cortez and I knew immediately it wasn't. The soul of Cortez was trapped back in that place where I'd gone.

"Rooster couldn't," I said. "Now who the hell are you?" Cortez's body slid up closer. "Smart boy. Good boy. Your daddy's son." He swung the torch close to me. I spun and backed up. So did Riley. "Rooster couldn't, but don't worry. I'll crack you open when the quake begins and my shadows here will shred you into nothing."

I remembered what Cortez had said. Fight! "I'll crack you!" I cried. I leapt at Cortez's body, threw a huge punch that sort of bounced off Cortez's gut. His face laughed. He backed away. The Shadows moved in, wrapped fabric around my arms, bound them behind my back, and lifted me off the ground.

Another Shadow went after Riley and he fought for about two seconds before he was bound and pulled off the ground, too.

"Good attempt, boys. You've both got the Wilkins fighting spirit! And the Wilkins propensity to die so young."

"I will mess you up," I said, struggling against my binds.

Cortez's face closed in on mine. "Feel the earth move, Charlie? Release is coming soon." A big smile grew on the fat face. Then he spoke to the Shadows. "Throw them in the crypt with the Kelly girl."

They carried us through a dark hall and threw us into a room. Shreds unwound from the Shadows and kept both Riley and me bound up. The Shadows receded into the dark from where we'd come.

Riley shouted, "Paula!"

There she was, the murdered blonde girl from the newspaper, except in ghostly form. Unlike Mouse and Mattheson, I'd never seen her like this. She glowed vaguely in the corner of the crypt. Shreds bound her transparent form—legs, arms and neck—to the wall. A Shred wrapped around the bottom of her face, so she couldn't talk. I could tell from her eyes that she knew us.

Riley and I leaned against the dirt wall across from her. "We're going to get you out!" Riley shouted.

Cortez entered the room carrying the torch. He laughed. "You're not going to get anyone out." He smashed the pointed end of the torch into the dirt floor and it stood by itself. Then he began pulling candles out of his coat pocket.

The torch was bright enough that I could see up to the top of the room, or crypt, where we were. The ceiling was easily twenty feet above us, and seemed to be the roof of a wooden structure. *Is that part of the cottage?* I wondered.

Cortez's body made an octagon pattern with the candles. He muttered and giggled over one and then lit it. "We will take revenge on the fifth generation and reach into the sixth in a single day!"

"Revenge for what?" I spat.

Cortez's head twisted towards me at an unnatural angle. "For Judge Hays' sins. He took my life, so I take his again and again," Cortez's face hissed.

Suddenly things made sense.

"You're Yankee Jim Robinson!" I shouted.

"Good, smart boy! You hanged me for stealing a boat!"

"No," I shouted. "Maybe my great, great, great, great grandpa, or whatever, did, but I didn't do anything!"

"You have his blood, like your daddy did and like Paula Kelly did! And so you will die in his stead!"

Just then, above us, someone screamed, "Ow shit! We're coming dudes!" There was a huge crash, followed by another, followed by some serious cries of pain, definitely Mouse and Mattheson. "Don't worry, bros!" Mattheson shouted.

Cortez looked up. "What is this?" he cried. "Shadows, go!"

The three Shadows began to float up.

"One of you stay," Cortez's face said. "If this is some attempt to save Charlie Wilkins, the girl must be cut as soon as the quake comes. Unbind her. Prepare her. She cannot escape now."

The largest of the Shadows turned back and spun towards the spirit of Paula Kelly. The Shreds that bound her body and face unwound and slid away. Fabric at the ends of the Shadow's arms began to sizzle and whistle and reach for her. She screamed.

"Fifth generation, child of John Hays, you have eluded obliteration for decades. But now is your time to pay for the sins of your family," Cortez cried.

"She doesn't have sins! She's just a kid!" I shouted.

The Shadow pressed in on the spirit of Paula Kelly.

"I'm sorry, I'm sorry," her voice quivered.

The hissing tethers of Shadow reached toward her face. And that was it. Riley couldn't take it. "No," he said quietly.

"What?" I said.

"I'm going to go in. Distract the hippie," Riley whispered.

He rolled onto his back and spun so his head was aimed across the room. He nodded at me. He mouthed, "Do it!"

I nodded then just let out a big scream. "Ahhhhhhh!"

Yankee Jim inside Cortez and the Shadow both turned fast towards me. Just as they did, Riley kicked hard off the wall. The dude slid across the floor right underneath the Shadow, so that his head must've popped out on the other side at Paula Kelly's feet.

"In my mouth!" Riley shouted.

"Stop him!" Cortez cried.

"Oh!" Paula said. And sudden as lightning, the unbound Paula was a string of energy that dropped into Riley's mouth, and, I guess, down his throat, into the heart of him. Riley rolled himself up into a ball.

"Holy shit, yes!" I shouted.

"Goddamn these children!" screamed Yankee Jim in Cortez's body. He kicked Riley hard, but Riley only smiled.

And then the structure, where fire spread fast above us, shook again.

Upstairs, Wiz, Mouse and Mattheson made it into the room where Riley and I had gone through the floor. The wall had fallen because of the fire, which caused another wall to fall backwards. Mouse had to jump and roll not to be hit by a collapsing ceiling beam. Half the cottage was engulfed in flames and its heavy, 150-year-old framing began to lose integrity.

Wiz scanned the west end of the cottage with his night vision goggles, but they didn't provide smoke vision, unfortunately. Then he saw the hole in the floor. "They must've gone down there!" He pointed. Right as he did, two giant Shadows rose from the hole.

"Shit!" Mattheson cried.

Mouse yanked the Stock Shock out of his pants. He zapped the closest one, which unloosed a few Shreds from its side, but did little else. But then a burning beam fell onto its back and it completely went up in flame. The energy in the Shreds released, sang, slid out the open part of the room.

"Everyone grab a burning board. We can set these buttholes on fire!" Wiz shouted.

"Should we go down the hole?" Mattheson asked.

"Yeah!" Mouse cried.

At that moment, one side of a heavy, structural timber above let loose. It swung down like a pendulum on a pivot and crashed hard into Mattheson's backside. The force sent him hurtling through the air and through a wall to Wiz's right. They heard him scream as he seemingly fell for seconds.

Back in the crypt, Yankee-in-Cortez was out of his mind. He ignored the explosions above. Riley clenched in a ball below him. "I shall gladly stomp the life out of this one!" He lifted his booted foot above Riley's big skull.

"No!" I cried. "Take me! I'm the sixth generation!"

"I'll get to you, Wilkins," Yankee hissed.

Suddenly there was crash from above. Cortez's body bent back and looked up in time to see a screaming Mattheson tumbling through the air. There was no time to move. Mattheson crashed head first into Cortez's broad chest. The fat hippie's body dropped flat backwards and the back of his large skull bounced heavily on the stone floor.

Luckily, the hippie's body cushioned Mattheson's fall. "I'm alive!" Mattheson shouted. He sat up on Cortez's chest and pumped his fists above his head "Hey, bros!" He looked down at Cortez's unconscious body. "Sorry dude," Mattheson said. Mattheson had, in fact, knocked Cortez out cold, and therefore Yankee Jim.

The Shadow that had been about to shred Paula reached for Mattheson.

"Look out!" I shouted.

Above us Wiz tried to set fire to the other Shadow that had gone after them, and Mouse, who was watching over the edge, jumped. "I'm coming down!" he screamed. He landed on the Shadow that threatened Mattheson and set fire to it with his two-by-four. He rolled off the thing's back as fire rushed through the matted fabric, releasing the Shreds. "Yeah, you sick bitch! Take that shit!" he cried.

Above, Wiz swung at the last Shadow, which hovered over the open crypt. His final swing hit pay dirt. The Shadow went up in flames! The sweet glow of Shreds rose into the air. But the momentum of his swing also took Wiz over the side. He flipped through the air. We all screamed. Mattheson jumped to his right and caught Wiz in his arms. They both tumbled and crashed into the poor beaten body of the hippie Cortez.

"Whoa. Glad that dude is built like a butter biscuit," Mouse said.

"Hey! Get me and Riley loose," I shouted.

While Mattheson and Wiz shook out the cobwebs and made it back to their feet, Mouse leaned over and carefully burned the Shred-bounds off me and Riley using the flaming two-by-four.

As soon as Mouse was done, I leapt up. Riley did too. A big smile spread across his pumpkin head. Yeah, Paula was clearly back where she felt good (right in the middle of Riley).

"Okay," I said. "Now how the shit do we get out of here?"

We all moved to the middle of the crypt and looked up. Fires burned the cottage. So intense. But that was our way out. The walls up to the cottage and ground level were made of rock. There were big stretches of sheer stone with little to grab on to, but also shelves of rock that we could stand on if we managed to get our asses up to them. If we knew how to rock climb like pros, seemed like we'd get out no problem. Of course, we were just scrawny eighth graders, for the most part. All of us except Riley, who had the growing ghost power of Paula inside him.

I turned to Riley. "Riley . . . I mean, Paula. Do you think you could climb up to those flat spots and maybe pull us up between them?"

"Hi Charlie," Riley's face said. It smiled. "I don't know!"

Then, without a hiccup, up the damn wall our girl Paula went. Riley looked like some kind of fat boy ninja scaling Mount Midoriyama. He got up to the first ledge, maybe ten feet up, slid onto his gut, and reached down. He pulled Mattheson up first. Then Mattheson lay down a few feet away and he pulled Mouse up. Riley pulled Wiz. As Riley got Wiz up to the top, Mattheson reached for me. Then he screamed like a little girl.

"Charlie! Shit, bro! Hippie!"

I spun around just in time to catch a huge, thunderous backhand to my face. The blow sent me flying across the room. I crashed up against the wall and fell to the floor. I was totally stunned. My eyes watered so bad, I couldn't even really see him, except it seemed like he was pointing something at me.

"Dude. The hippie has a knife," Mouse said.

"Don't any of you bastards move," Cortez's face said. "Or I butcher Charlie Wilkins right now."

"Who are you, man?" Mouse cried.

Cortez didn't answer. He spoke to me. "You of the sixth generation, Charlie Wilkins, descendant of John Hays . . ."

"Oh shit!" Wiz shouted, just figuring out what I already knew, "Hungry ghost! The hippie is seriously possessed!"

"You will take the place of Paula Kelly and I, Yankee Jim Robinson, will have my fifth victory over the Hays line, and then I will fade away."

I pushed myself off the floor. Blinked tears out of my eyes.

"Run, Charlie," Mouse shouted. But there was no place to run.

Yankee Jim reached out and grabbed my shirt collar. He pulled me in tight and breathed heavy, dead air on my face. "Prepare to die, young Wilkins," he hissed.

I struggled, pals. I tried to push him away, but Cortez's body was too heavy.

"That's right," Yankee Jim said. "Fight me. Fight for your life." He pressed the blade against my cheek. It bit.

"Fuck you," I said, and I figured that was the end for me, pals, and I was probably crying (okay, I was totally crying).

But right then, a flash of light momentarily ignited, cracked like lightning in the small space between my face and Cortez's big chest. It stunned Yankee. He let go of me and stumbled backwards. Suddenly between us stood the shimmering image of the boy, Rooster. The earth rumbled around us, releasing energy. Rooster burned bright. He became so clear, he looked substantial, human. He leaned in close to me, backing me against the wall.

"Your father saves you," he whispered. "Your friends risk all to save the Kelly girl. My Uncle Yankee sends me to hell. I'm cold, but I will not go with him no more."

"Get out of here Rooster, or I'll shred you, too!" Yankee roared.

Rooster turned to him. Another rumble spread through the rock and earth around us. Rooster grew brighter. "Ever since I took my last breath, you make me follow, you make me hurt. I won't hurt no more. I am over."

The earth shook heavily. Yankee began to laugh. "Too late. The quake is on us. Wilkins dies."

"No," Rooster said.

The quaking earth grew loud. Yankee Jim sliced at Rooster with the knife. The blade went through him, did no damage at all. Rooster smiled.

"Isn't it foolish to take human form at a time like this, Uncle?"

"I will get you for this," Yankee Jim hissed.

"I will be long gone!"

And Rooster in a moment turned into a bolt of energy. He fired into Cortez's eye. There was a terrible splatting sound, like an egg hitting the kitchen floor. Yankee screamed, dropped the knife, and collapsed. The body of Cortez convulsed. A hiss of steam poured from Cortez's mouth and nose. I pasted myself against the shaking wall. A soul rose like a thin mist from Cortez's body. It hovered for a moment, took a decrepit human form. The ghost figure of an old dude from the West glared at me, shivered. "I will come for you again, Wilkins," it snarled. And then the ghost of Yankee Jim Robinson disappeared.

"Yeah!" Mattheson screamed from above. "You killed the hippie!"

"Oh no. Cortez," I whispered. But there wasn't time to mourn.

The earth totally roiled. I looked up. The other dudes lay on the shaking ledge ten feet above, their eyes wide. "We have to get out of here!" I screamed.

"We can't make it out by going up," Wiz said. "It's all fire now."

"Oh, wait. I know a different way," Riley's face said.

"How?" I shouted.

"The tunnels," Riley said. "Where Rooster and Yankee come from. We can go through."

The Olivenhain Cottage above us collapsed, sending sparks and flaming shards of shattered wood down on us. The earth shuddered and moaned.

"Show us how right now!" I cried.

CHAPTER THIRTY-FIVE

Just as the sun rose on the eastern horizon, Paula Kelly, a girl who had been dead thirty-five years, who happened to be hanging out in the body of a boy named Riley, led us through ancient underground tunnels to the safety of Olivenhain Cemetery. In between the old cowboy gravestones, we clung to the ground and screamed through the biggest Encinitas-area earthquake since 1892. Dudes, it was intense.

When the shaking stopped, we all stared at each other for like five minutes straight.

I looked up at the Olivenhain Cottage, which was still burning, which hadn't attracted police or the fire department, probably because the earthquake did a lot of damage in a lot of places, and said, "I want to go home."

255

We all did, except for Riley, really. He didn't have much of a home and he had a ghost girl inside of him. I told him to at least get away from the cottage.

We all said these super awkward goodbyes. I was so exhausted I think I told Mattheson, "Love you, man." But, seriously, I sort of meant it. Four days before I hated everyone, you know? By the time we got out of that crypt, I had four friends I'd pretty much fight anybody for. Then we left the cemetery.

And, guess what? Some of us got into trouble for being out all night.

Mattheson's mom, for instance, noticed he wasn't in his bed in the morning. She, for the first time in history, grounded him. Poor dude wasn't allowed to join her and her best friend Maura for pizza night at the Blue Ribbon the following Monday. She did bring him back some pizza, though, so that's good.

Some of us got some new cred.

Mouse's five brothers saw Mouse in a new light. He was no longer the little dipshit runt of the family. He was the boy capable of such mayhem somebody might lose his car and his pants in some rad explosion involving terrifying, flying, blood-sucking rags. Yeah, Barton was a little pissed at him, until Mouse reported the car stolen. After a short investigation, the cops said the Pinto had been destroyed by meth heads who had also managed to burn down the historic Olivenhain Cottage during the earthquake (using both the Pinto and some kind of solar panel and battery they were trying to cook drugs with—our first attempt at a ghost trap was mistaken for meth gear, ha ha). Barton received some insurance money. He bought a Camaro.

Wiz returned to some serious changes. When he got back to the glass palace that housed his family, he found a stern-looking Gramps sitting in the living room. Some shit had gone down while Wiz was off battling ghouls. His mom, worried about the fight he had with his father, went to see him in his room and discovered that Wiz had "run away." She apparently lost her mind. It had been a long time coming, but this series of events—Mr. Wisniewski threatening military school, drinking gin all night, scaring the shit out of Wiz so he took off during ghosting hour— broke Wiz's mom. She threw Mr. Wisniewski out of the house and would begin divorce proceedings shortly. Wiz was glad. Dude legitimately despised his father. Gramps was the only one who knew Wiz had actually been in action, not just acting out. Gramps invited Wiz up to his shack the next day. He shouted at Wiz for engaging in crazy-ass behaviors, driving his truck, stealing and losing his photo- voltaic cells and his Stock Shock and his bug zapper (all lost in the Olivenhain fire). Kid was clearly chasing ghosts deep into the night! But all Wiz could think was, "I'm ready to do it again." That Sunday evening he called me up to let me know he'd made this website, *Strange Times*, to honor my dad and to help track paranormal activity wherever it might crop up. How dope is that? The site has tipped us off to huge shit we've been chasing down ever since.

Late the next night, after going to the beach (Paula still inside him) Riley finally went back to Hoover and Memaw's apartment. His grandparents were asleep and obviously not looking for him. He stretched out on the couch and began to drift off (dude hadn't really slept in three days at that point). Paula, without warning, slid out of him. "What are you doing?" he whispered.

She stretched herself thin and lay on top of him like a cool sheet. She said, "I'm a dead girl. I know that. There's a door I've been scared of, but I'm going through it now. I think Rooster did. If he can do it, so can I."

"Don't go," Riley said.

"I'll miss you," Paula said. She kissed Riley. She floated off him, up, smiled and evaporated.

Our boy Riley cried like a baby, because he lost his first girlfriend, who had actually been a part of him. A couple hours later he stopped though. He went out on the balcony of the apartment and looked out over Encinitas. He said it looked like home to him, not just because Paula had grown up here, but because he had a new crew. He felt like his life was beginning again.

In some ways, I was the luckiest of the crew. My mom got home after her nursing shift the morning of the quake and realized I wasn't in bed. She panicked. She called the cops and searched all over the neighborhood. When I came rolling up on my SE after the quake (there was damage everywhere), she just broke down and cried and cried. Lindsey, when she saw me, cried and hugged me, too. I told them I was working on the same science project that I was the night before and I was just at a friend's house. I said, "We passed out while writing the report."

Mom said, "I can't lose you. Don't scare me like that ever again. Please!"

She didn't ground me or anything. Here's what's weird, though, pals. Late in the day I rode over to Mouse's to pick up my back pack (I'd left it there). The walkie-talkie from Cortez was still in it. On my bike ride home, it came to life.

"Charlie Wilkins, you out there?" the thing said.

Nearly scared me to death. I almost threw the bag into a bush. But then I answered. Cortez wasn't dead.

The following day, Sunday, I woke up early, got on my SE and rode all the way out to Poway. I found Cortez's place backed up against the mountain. He was waiting for me. He had a patch covering his left eye. He made me some of that shitty red tea. He told me he woke up while the walls were coming down. He told me Rooster—that crazy ghost—woke him up as the earth was shaking, led him out through the tunnels. Cortez said, "I watched the kid enter the light. Most beautiful thing I ever saw, little dude. With my right eye, because my left eye is smushed!"

Pals, I can't tell you how relieved I still am that Cortez didn't die. He still helps the Strange Times crew from time to time (he got Riley some ointment, too).

That day, I had one big question for him, though. It was about my dad.

Cortez sighed. He nodded. He said, "Like I told you on the beach, little dude, no one is ever gone. Everything changes. All matter changes. But energy can't be destroyed. No one is ever gone from you."

"So, was Dad with me or with us at all?" I asked.

Cortez paused for a moment then said, "Hell if I know, buddy. I surely don't doubt it. I just don't know for sure. All I do know about that day is I only applied about half my anti-possession ointment because you guys showed up at my house in the middle of me doing it and that son of a bitch Yankee Jim got in my body as soon as I got to Olivenhain. Now the treasure map I've been working on for years, which your dad borrowed from me and you wouldn't return to me . . ."

"I thought Dad didn't want you to have it!" I said.

"He was going to use it to take down Yankee Jim. He wasn't trying to keep it away from me. But then, you know, he disappeared and he set up that damn cloaking parrot . . ." Cortez said. "Anyhoo, I lost track of the loot that bitch Yankee stole from my family many generations ago."

"I'm so sorry, man," I said.

Cortez shrugged. "I still got my trailer! And one good eye! And I got you, right? Maybe you and me can go after that treasure again? Wilkinses are natural investigators. What do you think?"

I wasn't sure right at that moment, pals.

As I was leaving, Cortez warned me that, no matter what, I had to deal with Yankee Jim sooner than later, because that "ornery ass ghoul" would come after me again and again. "He's weak as shit now. Probably will be for a few years. You can find him at the Whaley House down in San Diego, where the guest book came from. But be warned! Place has the worst, darkest energy in the damn world. So, you little dudes be careful."

"Dudes?" I asked.

"You and your crew. Your posse. What do you call yourselves?" Cortez asked.

"Strange Times," I said. "Yeah, definitely. Strange Times."

Over the next few weeks, as the dudes and I worked on our actual science project, which Riley insisted be about how frogs are affected by synthetic chemicals and how the chemicals cause them to grow multiple legs and wangs—pretty weird shit (we got a B minus on it, by the way, because the morning of the presentation Mouse's brothers stole a bunch of our multi-wanged frog models), I thought a lot about what Cortez said, how energy can't ever be destroyed. I thought a lot about what had happened to me, how I'd nearly died. I thought about how I felt when I was being carried through that terrible tunnel. I am sure, okay? I'm pretty sure.

I think my dad is out there some place.

Anyway . . .

CHAPTER THIRTY-SIX

So, yeah. This thing, our battle with the evil spirit Yankee Jim Robinson, has been going on for quite a while. Last night was the fifth time we'd tried to get him in the last couple of years. We broke into the Whaley House with a serious high-tech ghost trap Wiz built.

I led the way through the cellar door. I carried a magnum flashlight.

Wiz followed me. Riley followed Wiz carrying the Mel Meter. Mouse and Mattheson were behind (Mattheson with the trap).

At the top of the steps, Mouse leaned over Riley's elbow. He said, "That thing's not working, bro. Not at all. No light. How are you going to see the meter?"

"There's supposed to be a light on the Mel?" Riley asked.

"We've been over this," Wiz said. "It only lights up if it detects something."

"Shh," I said to all of them. I focused the magnum's beam on the door into the dining room. "This way."

Just then Mattheson made it up the stairs, struggling with the weight of the trap in his arms. "Hey. You smell, like, a fart smell?" Mattheson asked.

"You always smell that," Mouse said.

I pushed through a door and walked carefully into the dining room. Darkness. Dust floating in the beam of my light. The others followed right behind. Once we were all in the dining room, I held up my hand. Wiz stopped. But Riley didn't. Mouse didn't. They all ran into each other.

"Watch for Charlie's signal," Wiz hissed.

I'd stopped because I'd heard a creak. A floorboard. Then, I heard a rustle, like a faint wind through the curtains, except the windows had to be closed for the night. There couldn't be a breeze. "Do you hear something?" I asked.

"What? What do you hear, dude?" Riley whispered back.

It wasn't a breeze in the curtains. It was a whisper, a voice. "Somebody's speaking," I said. "I think."

"Yeah, me," Mouse said. "All of us."

"Shh," I whispered.

And then, through rooms surrounding us, a ghostly voice drifted in the dark, "Hello, boys. You've come for me, I see . . ."

I was startled for a second. Spirit voices aren't usually so clear. I hoped to shit he hadn't gotten strong again. "Yankee Jim, you bastard. Is that you?"

He didn't answer. The floorboards creaked again, though. I shined the light at the ceiling, then a hiss, like steam escaping a pipe, rose from the other side of the dining room. I aimed the light there. Nothing.

"Is that you Yankee? I'm sorry I called you a bastard. I want to end the trouble between us," I said.

"Yes. We come in peace," Mouse shouted.

The Mel Meter in Riley's hand lit up. "Hey look!" Riley said. "It turned on!"

"Are you here, Yankee?" I shouted to the air. Then I turned to Mattheson and whispered, "Turn on the trap." He pressed a button on the tank and the oil emitted a weak, purple glow.

Then the Mel Meter got even brighter. Wiz turned and stared at it. "That's not right. It's not supposed to do that. It doesn't have enough battery power to . . ."

At that moment, a large oriental vase slid off the fireplace mantle to our left. I spun and caught its movement in the beam of my magnum. The vase hovered in the air and shivered.

"Check it out," I whispered.

"Holy shit," said Mouse. "Here we go again."

Slowly, the vase moved through the air towards us. The Mel Meter glowed brighter and brighter, until its green light became almost blinding. It began to buzz.

"What am I supposed to do with this?" Riley cried. "It's burning my hand! It's burning!"

"Yankee Jim? Are you moving the vase?" I called.

A laugh echoed all around us.

"We're here to end this!" I shouted. "Manifest so we can kick your . . . bury the hatchet. Show yourself."

The vase slowly moved across the room, lit by the blinding Mel. It floated until it was directly over Mattheson. "Dude, it's totally going to fall on my head," he said, looking up.

"Talk to us!" I shouted.

The vase rotated slowly, as if tied by a string to the ceiling. The Mel Meter sizzled and sparked. Riley whimpered. Mattheson, holding tight to our glowing trap, slowly stepped to his left, out from underneath the thing. The vase followed and positioned itself above him again.

"Shit!" Mattheson whimpered.

"What do you want, Yankee?" I cried.

Suddenly, my flashlight and the Mel Meter both went dark.

"Uh oh," said Mouse.

The voice whispered, "I want you dead."

The words hung in the air for a moment.

"Just Charlie, or all of us?" asked Mouse.

"Everyone, everyone, everyone," the voice hissed.

In the dark, the vase crashed onto Mattheson's head. He screamed, dropped the trap. We slid in the oil, ran away, skated off through the night before the cops got there.

Damn that bastard, Yankee!

But yeah, know what? This crew, the Strange Times crew, is dope. We talk to aliens. We've shared burgers with demons. We rode on the back of a goddamn sea monster!

I guess we have Yankee Jim to thank for all of that.

Still, one day, we're going to get him.

THE END